'I got myself into this,' Maggie said. 'I will handle it.'

'If you think that I would allow you to wander off into the sunset with a child of mine, think again.'

Maggie's eyes widened as she realised what Jack was saying, but there was more.

'If you think I would allow a child of mine to be swallowed up in the midst of *your* family—that is simply not on the cards.'

'I would never deny you access to your child.'

'And do you think you're strong enough to hold out against your father, Maggie, if he sees things differently? I don't. There's only one thing to do,' Jack concluded. 'The sooner you marry me the better.'

Lindsay Armstrong was born in South Africa, but now lives in Australia with her New Zealand-born husband and their five children. They have lived in nearly every state of Australia, and have tried their hand at some unusual—for them—occupations, such as farming and horse-training—all grist to the mill for a writer! Lindsay started writing romances when their youngest child began school and she was left feeling at a loose end. She is still doing it and loving it.

Recent titles by the same author:

THE MILLIONAIRE'S MARRIAGE CLAIM
A BRIDE FOR HIS CONVENIENCE
THE AUSTRALIAN'S CONVENIENT BRIDE

THE RICH MAN'S VIRGIN

BY
LINDSAY ARMSTRONG

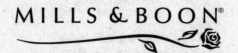
MILLS & BOON®

First published in Great Britain 2005
Harlequin Mills & Boon Limited,
Eton House, 18-24 Paradise Road, Richmond, Surrey TW9 1SR

© Lindsay Armstrong 2005

ISBN 0 263 84190 1

Set in Times Roman 10½ on 12 pt.
01-1005-44497

Printed and bound in Spain
by Litografía Rosés, S.A., Barcelona

PROLOGUE

MAGGIE TRENT and Jack McKinnon conducted rather unreal conversations at times.

Why this should be so had something to do with the unreal nature of their relationship, Maggie felt. Nothing ever went according to plan in their lives. Their first meeting had been sheer coincidence, their second meeting sheer disaster, their third meeting should have had labels stuck all over it shouting, 'Spoilt, little rich girl determined to get her own way'—according, at first anyway, to Jack.

They'd parted after that extended meeting, not well, and determined never wittingly to come together again.

Yet just under a year later Maggie began one of her unreal conversations with Jack McKinnon on the subject of their two-month-old son who had started out life known as Trent/McKinnon—it had been written on his wrist band and on the label on his cot. They'd dispensed with the stroke after a week but stuck with the Trent McKinnon.

The gist of their conversation was this.

'This is a very proper baby,' Maggie said seriously one evening.

'I never thought he was a porcelain doll.'

'No. I mean, he's very well organized. He does everything by the book.'

Jack frowned. 'He's only eight weeks old. How can you say that?'

Maggie was attractively dressed in slim white trousers and a floral seersucker jacket trimmed with green. Her dark gold hair was tied back with a green scrunchie; her green eyes were clear and she was sitting beside a cot.

Trent McKinnon was asleep in the cot.

'I'll tell you. He adapted himself to a four-hourly schedule right from the start under extremely difficult circumstances. He burps beautifully and he mostly sleeps between feeds just as the book says he should. He has one wakeful period, after his two p.m. feed, where he'll accept conversation and he quite appreciates being carried around for a bit. He now sleeps through the eight hours from ten p.m. to six a.m.'

'Is there anything he doesn't do by the book?' Jack asked with a grin. 'He sounds almost too good to be true.'

Maggie considered. 'He hates having his hair washed. He gets extremely upset, but even that isn't going against the book exactly. They do warn that some babies hate it.'

'Screams blue murder?'

'Yes. Otherwise—' she shrugged '—there's nothing he doesn't do very correctly.'

'What are you worried about, then?'

Maggie stared down at her sleeping son with her heart in her eyes. 'I can't help thinking he would be horrified if he knew how—irregular—his situation was.'

She looked up and their gazes clashed.

'Born out of wedlock, you mean?' he said, and for a fleeting moment his mouth hardened. 'That was your choice, Maggie.'

She inclined her head. 'That was before—all sorts

of things happened,' she said quietly and ran her fingers along the arm of her chair. 'That was definitely before I came to appreciate the reality of having a baby and what a baby deserves.'

CHAPTER ONE

MAGGIE TRENT sold real estate.

None of her family or friends particularly appreciated her job, although her mother was supportive, until Mary Donaldson of Tasmania got engaged to Crown Prince Frederik of Denmark and it was revealed that she had worked in a real estate office.

From then on, everyone looked at Maggie Trent with renewed interest, even a little spark of 'the world could be your oyster too'!

In fact, the world could have been Maggie's oyster anyway, had she wanted it. She came from a very wealthy background. At twenty-three she was a golden blonde, attractive, always stylish and well groomed.

Nevertheless, she also had a well-developed commercial instinct and a flair for her job in the form of matching the right people to the right properties plus a very real 'eye' for the potential in houses that many missed.

This came from the Bachelor of Arts degree she'd done at university along with courses in architecture and draughting, as well as her natural interest in people and her ability to get along with them. She'd been born with great taste.

If she had a creed it was that nothing was unsaleable.

She was enjoying her life and her career far too much, especially with the property boom going the way it was, to contemplate marriage, although there was at least one man in her life who wished she would—not a prince of any designation, however.

But Maggie had two goals. One was to prove that she was a highly successful businesswoman in her own right. She had visions of opening her own agency one day. The other was to allow no man to make her feel inferior because she was a woman. Both these ambitions had been nurtured by a difficult relationship with her father, a powerful, wealthy, often arrogant man who believed she was wasting her time working at all and equated real-estate agents with used-car salesmen.

It was undoubtedly—she didn't try to hide it from herself—this mindset that saw her take such exception to Jack McKinnon, wealthy property developer, with such disastrous results—not that she'd ever intended to deprive him of his liberty!

She couldn't deny that was how it had turned out, though. Nor had the fact that she'd been deprived of *her* liberty at the same time seemed to hold much weight with him at all. In fact, he'd ascribed some really weird motives to it all that still annoyed her to think of…

Anyway, it all started one sunny Sunday afternoon.

She and Tim Mitchell were sipping coffee and listening to an excellent jazz band amongst a lively crowd on a marina boardwalk. Her relationship with Tim was fairly casual. They did a lot of things together, but Maggie always drew the line at getting further involved. Truth be told this was placing undue strain on Tim, but he did a good job of hiding it.

'Who's that?' Maggie asked idly. She was feeling relaxed and content. She'd sold a house that morning that was going to earn her a rather nice, fat commission.

Tim glanced over his shoulder at the new arrivals that had caught Maggie's attention and drew an excited breath.

'Jack McKinnon,' he said. 'You know—the property developer.'

Maggie stared at the man. She did know the name and the man, but only by reputation.

Jack McKinnon was a millionaire many times over and amongst other things he headed the company that was developing new housing estates in what Maggie thought of as 'her patch', the Gold Coast hinterland.

If she was honest, and she was, Maggie disapproved of the kind of housing estates Jack McKinnon developed. She saw it as tearing up of the rural land that had always been the Coast's buffer zone. The area where you could own a few acres, run a few horses, breed llamas or whatever took your fancy; the green zone that was a retreat for many from the high-rise and suburbia of the rest of the Coast.

Now, thanks to Jack McKinnon and others, part of that green zone was disappearing and thousands of cheek-by-jowl 'little boxes' were taking its place.

Unfortunately, the reality of it was that the Coast's population was burgeoning. Not only did it offer a good climate and great beaches, but its proximity to Brisbane, the state's capital, also made it desirable and future urban development was inevitable.

Doesn't mean to say I have to like the people involved in doing it and making a fortune out of it at the same time, she mused.

'Do you know him?' she asked Tim as Jack

McKinnon and his party, two women and another man, selected a table not far away and sat down.

'I went to school with him, but he's a few years older. Bumped into him a couple of times since. He's a Coast boy who really made good,' Tim said with pride.

Maggie opened her mouth to demolish the likes of Jack McKinnon, then decided to hold her peace. Tim was sweet and good company. At twenty-nine he was a dentist with his own practice. With his engaging ways and a passion for all things orthodontic, and the prices dentists charged these days, she had no doubt he would 'really make good' as well, although perhaps not on the scale of Jack McKinnon.

It was on the tip of her tongue to ask Tim what the man was like, but she realized suddenly that she couldn't fathom why she wanted to know, and she puzzled over that instead.

It came to her there was definitely an aura to him that she found a little surprising.

His dark fair hair streaked lighter by the sun fell in his eyes. He would be over six feet, she judged, slim but broad-shouldered and he looked lithe and light on his feet.

Unlike many of the 'white shoe' brigade, Gold Coast identities, particularly entrepreneurs, who had over the years earned the sobriquet because of their penchant for flashy dressing, Jack McKinnon was very casually dressed with not a gold chain in sight.

He wore jeans, brown deck shoes, a white T-shirt and a navy pullover slung over his shoulders.

There was also a pent-up dynamism about him that easily led you to imagine him flying a plane through the sound barrier, crewing a racing yacht, climbing

Mount Everest, hunting wild animals and testing himself to the limit—rather than developing housing estates.

As these thoughts chased through her mind, perhaps the power of her concentration on him seeped through to him because he turned abruptly and their gazes clashed.

A little flare of colour entered Maggie's cheeks and Jack McKinnon raised an ironic eyebrow. Even then she was unable to tear her gaze away. Somehow or other he had her trapped, she thought chaotically as more colour poured into her cheeks. Then he noticed Tim and instant recognition came to him.

That was how Tim and Maggie came to join Jack's party.

She tried to resist, but Tim's obvious delight made it difficult. Nor was there any real reason for her to feel uneasy amongst Jack McKinnon's party, at first.

Her slim black linen dress and high-heeled black patent sandals were the essence of chic. Her thick dark gold hair fell to her shoulders when loose, but was tied back with a velvet ribbon today. Her golden skin was smooth and luminous.

She was, in other words, as presentable as the other two women. Nor were they unfriendly, although they were both the essence of sophistication. One, a flashing brunette, was introduced as Lia Montalba, the other, Nordic fair, as Bridget Pearson. The second man, Paul Wheaton, was a lawyer who acted for the McKinnon Corporation, but who was paired with whom was hard to say.

The conversation was light-hearted. They discussed the music. The McKinnon party had spent the night out on Jack's boat cruising the Broadwater, and had some fishy tales to tell, mainly about the ones that got away.

The man himself—why did Maggie think of him thus? she wondered—had a deep, pleasant voice, a lurking grin and a wicked sense of humour.

All the same, Maggie did feel uneasy and it was all to do with Jack McKinnon, she divined. Not that he paid her much attention, so was she still stinging inwardly from that ironically raised eyebrow and her curious inability to tear her gaze from his?

Well, if he thought her scrutiny was the prelude to her making a pass at him, if that was why he was now virtually ignoring her, he was mistaken and she was perfectly content to be ignored.

Or was she?

It occurred to her that what he was doing was a deliberate insult and before much longer everyone was going to realize it, to her humiliation. Her blood began to boil. Who did he think he was?

Then he trained his grey gaze on her and said musingly, 'Maggie Trent. David Trent's daughter, by any chance?'

She hesitated. 'Yes,' she replied briefly.

'*The* David Trent?' Lia asked, her big dark eyes wide. 'Ultra-wealthy, from a long line of distinguished judges and politicians, grazier, racehorse owner, champion yachtsman?'

Maggie shrugged.

'Maggie doesn't like to trade on her father,' Tim murmured.

What an understatement, Maggie marvelled, considering how stormy their father/daughter relationship had sometimes been.

'Lucky you, Maggie,' Paul commented.

'Yes,' Jack McKinnon agreed. 'Do you actually do anything useful, Maggie? Not that one could blame you if you didn't.'

Even Tim, obviously a fan of Jack McKinnon, did a double take.

As for Maggie, she stared at Jack out of sparkling green eyes—green eyes sparkling with rage, that was.

'I knew there was one good reason not to like you,' she said huskily. 'I detest the little boxes you build and the way you destroy the landscape to do so. Now I have another reason. Wealthy, powerful men who are completely in love with themselves mean absolutely nothing to me, Mr McKinnon.'

She got up and walked away.

She had a rostered day off on Monday, and she spent the morning with her mother.

In contrast to her sometimes stormy relationship with her father, Maggie adored her mother.

In her middle forties, Belle Trent looked years younger. Her straight dark hair was streaked with grey, but it was so glossy and beautifully cut many younger women envied it. With her fine dark eyes and slim figure she was essentially elegant. She was also a busy person; she did a great deal of charity work.

Yet there were times when Maggie sensed a current of sadness in her mother, but it was an enigmatic kind of sadness Maggie couldn't really fathom. She knew it had to do with her father, that at times their marriage was strained, but for no real reason Maggie could put her finger on.

Belle never complained and there was never any suggestion that it might break up, although, with a certain cynicism, Maggie sometimes wondered whether neither her mother nor her father could face the Herculean task of sorting out a divorce settlement.

But that Monday morning as she had coffee with her mother at a chic Sanctuary Cove pavement café, Maggie had something else on her mind.

'Do you know anything about the McKinnon Corporation and Jack McKinnon, Mum?'

Belle stirred sugar into her latte. 'Uh—I believe he's a bit of a whizkid. He started with nothing, I heard. Somehow or other he persuaded a bank to finance his first development and he hasn't looked back since. He now not only develops the estate but he has a construction company that builds many of the houses. Of course housing estates are not the only string to his bow.'

'No?'

Belle shook her head. 'No,' she said. 'Once he made his first few millions he diversified into boat-building. McKinnon Catamarans have taken off. If you looked through this marina—' she waved a hand towards the forest of masts and all sorts of boats moored in the Sanctuary Cove marina just across the road from the shopping and restaurant precinct '—you'd probably find quite a few.'

'So, if he started with nothing, he must be—clever,' Maggie hazarded.

'I believe he's one of *those*.' Belle wrinkled her nose. 'You know, the kind of gifted person with a lot of foresight and a lot of drive who is always going to make good. I don't believe he's at all ostentatious about it, though.'

'Hmm…'

Belle raised an eyebrow. 'Do you know him?'

'I met him. Yesterday, as it happens. He was rather rude to me.'

Her mother blinked. 'Why?'

'I have no idea.' Maggie frowned. 'How come you know so much about him?'

'Your aunt Elena has decided to put him on her list of eligible bachelors,' Belle said ruefully.

They stared at each other, then started to laugh. Elena Chadwick was actually Belle's cousin. She'd never married yet she wrote a column in a weekly magazine dispensing advice on all sorts of marital problems. When anyone took issue with her lack of experience on the subject, she protested that it was her unbiased views that were invaluable. She was a great promoter of innovative methods for 'holding onto your man'.

She also kept and updated quarterly, to the delight of her readers, a ten most eligible bachelors' list; the other noteworthy thing about Elena Chadwick was her talent for unearthing all sorts of unusual facts about people.

'If I didn't dislike him so much,' Maggie said, still gurgling with laughter, 'I'd feel sorry for him with Elena in hot pursuit! On the other hand, I have no doubt that he can look after himself.'

'What's he like?'

Maggie considered. 'I don't know, but he could be the kind of man women ride off with into the sunset without giving it a great deal of thought. Some women.'

'Hmm…' Belle said, echoing her daughter's earlier *Hmm* of doubt and reservation, but accompanied by a searching little look that Maggie missed.

*   *   *

When she got home later, Maggie closed her front door and took her usual few deep breaths of sheer appreciation of her home.

It was a two-storeyed villa overlooking a lovely golf course on Hope Island. It had a small garden, a conservatory dining room overlooking a fountain and she'd inherited it from her paternal grandmother. She'd also inherited some of the lovely pieces that furnished and decorated it.

She'd been very fond of her father's mother. Everyone told her she took after Leila Trent, not only in looks but personality although, curiously, this was the one area where they'd failed to agree. Leila had always insisted that if Margaret Leila Trent took after anyone, it was her father, David Trent.

'But we never do anything but fight!' Maggie protested, more than once. 'Well, not always, but you know what I mean.'

'That's because, underneath, you're so much alike,' Leila insisted. 'Oh, you've got your mother's more gentle genes to balance it, darling, but essentially you're a Trent and, whatever else you might like to say about your father, that means you have a lot of drive and a lot of nerve. Your grandfather was much the same.'

Once, Maggie voiced the opinion that she should have been a boy—to gain her father's approval anyway.

Leila looked at her piercingly. 'Don't go down that road, Maggie. Your mother has and—' She stopped, then added slowly, 'You just be yourself.'

Leila would never elaborate on what she'd been about to say and six months ago she'd died peacefully in her sleep.

Maggie tossed her bag onto the settee and slipped off her shoes.

She'd managed to avoid Tim, although she'd spoken to him on the phone and accepted his apologies for what had happened. What she hadn't been able to accept was his complete bafflement over the incident.

'Jack's just—normally—not *like* that,' he said several times.

Oh, yes? she thought cynically, but she told Tim it wasn't his fault and said simply that she'd be in touch shortly.

'I hope that's not a 'don't call us, we'll call you' message, Maggie?'

Maggie said no, of course not, but now, as she padded out to water her garden in her bare feet, she frowned, because the fact was that since Sunday afternoon's incident she'd been curiously at odds with herself. She just couldn't put her finger on why this was so. Why her smooth, successful life she'd been enjoying so much was suddenly not so appealing to her any more.

It couldn't have anything to do with Jack McKinnon's insulting manner and words, surely?

After all, he'd completely misread her. He'd taken her for an idle little rich girl, a daddy's pet, so how on earth could that start her thinking along some strange lines?

Strange lines such as a sudden dissatisfaction to do with her relationship with Tim?

Not that you could call it much of a relationship, but there was the fact that Tim dearly wanted to make it into something more while she didn't, and she was suddenly feeling guilty about it.

It wasn't only that, though. To be tarred with the same brush as her father was extremely annoying. She might, according to her grandmother, have inherited some of her father's genes, but not, she devoutly hoped, his arrogance. She might have a fairly well-developed commercial instinct when it came to the property market, but a lot of people thought of her father as a ruthless businessman—she certainly wasn't ruthless.

As usual, her garden soothed her. She'd had no idea she possessed green fingers until she'd inherited her villa. In six months she'd transformed the small garden into a colourful showpiece. She grew roses and camellias, impatiens, petunias and daisies, yellow, pink and white. Her lawn was like green velvet and her herb garden provided basil, mint, coriander, rosemary, sage, parsley, thyme and oregano.

So she watered and pottered and pruned dead heads until both Tim Mitchell and Jack McKinnon faded from her mind, quite unaware that Jack 'the man' would raise his undeniably attractive head in the most unexpected way when she went back to work the following morning.

Maggie was the only agent not engaged with clients when an elderly couple walked into the office on Tuesday morning, so she took them under her wing and set about making her usual assessment of what kind of a property they wanted to buy. This could often be a tricky business, but with Sophie and Ernest Smith it proved to be more—it proved to be a marital war zone.

It transpired that they had sold their previous property, a house and eight acres, to a developer. Sophie had not been in favour of doing this at all and claimed she wasn't going to be happy anywhere else, anyway.

Ernest, with a lack of patience that indicated this battle had been fought many a time before, detailed to Maggie why he'd thought it was such a good idea at the time.

They were getting on and eight acres were quite a handful. Once developers got their eye on an area what option did you have but to sell out unless you relished the thought of being hemmed in by hundreds of houses? The price they'd been offered would assure a comfortable retirement...

'Yes,' Sophie Smith said grimly, 'but if you'd hung on as I suggested, we would have got a lot more for it!'

Ernest bristled. 'We weren't to know that, woman, and a bird in the hand is worth two in the bush!'

Maggie spent a few moments calming them down, then asked for more details. The Smiths were the first to be approached in their road by the developer, and the ones to sell out cheapest. Others in the road who had held out over a period of time had received better offers.

It was obvious to Maggie that, not only had Sophie really loved her property and not wanted to sell anyway, but that the higher prices some of her neighbours had attained were going to be a thorn in her flesh and a cause for discontent between her and her husband for the rest of their lives.

'Who was the developer?' she asked.

Ernest heaved a sigh. 'The McKinnon Corporation.'

As Maggie surveyed the two unhappy people before her once again her blood boiled directly on account of Jack McKinnon.

All the same, she might never have done anything about it had fate not intervened.

A few days later, she was doing a property assessment.

The owners had relocated to Melbourne over a year ago. They'd contacted her by phone with instructions to value the property with a view to putting it on the market and they'd posted her the keys.

The house, she discovered, showed every sign of not having been lived in for quite a time—it was distinctly unloved and it was a crying shame because it had obviously once been a beautiful home with loads of character. But the acreage was green and rolling, there were lovely trees on it and a delightful, secretive creek ran through it. A creek, she felt sure, you would find platypus playing in.

There was also a large brick shed. She left it to last to inspect and finally tore herself away from the creek to do so. The shed had two means of access: a set of double doors you could drive a vehicle through, but they were heavily barred and padlocked, and a stout wooden single door with a deadlock. She unlocked it and walked into the cavernous gloom of the building.

One corner of it had been converted into a rudimentary dwelling, she found, complete with kitchenette, bathroom and toilet. The kitchenette had a small two-burner stove. There were an old kettle and a couple of pots as well as some mismatched china and cutlery. The kitchen cupboard held some tinned food and dry goods, but there was little furniture, only a sagging settee and a Formica-topped table with four chairs. But there were, as she clicked a light switch then ran a tap, both electricity and water connected.

She made some notes and looked around again, but it was bare except for a large mound covered with tarpaulins in one corner. She was just about to investigate when the scamper of mice in the rafters caused her to grimace and decide against it.

That was when she heard a vehicle pull up outside. To her amazement, as she watched through the doorway, who should step out of the late-model Range Rover but Jack McKinnon?

She stared through the door wide-eyed, but there was no mistaking him as he stretched and looked around. He wore buff chinos and a dark green long-sleeved shirt with patch pockets, casually dressed again in other words, but still—how to put it?—a very compelling presence? Yes.

All the same— *Oh, no! No, you don't!* were her next sentiments. No way are you going to turn this little piece of heaven into a housing estate, Jack McKinnon.

She emerged from the shadows of the shed with an ominous expression on her face.

'Well, well,' he drawled as they came face to face, 'if it isn't little Miss Trent, green crusader and man-hater.'

He looked her up and down and decided, somewhat to his surprise, that if she were anyone but David Trent's daughter he would find her rather peachy despite her grim expression.

Peachy? he thought with an ironic twist of his lips. Where did that come from? You wouldn't exactly call—he dredged his mind for an example—Lia Montalba peachy. Svelte, stunning, sexy, sophisticated—yes, definitely that, but peachy? No. So why apply it to this girl? Did it indicate a succulent, fresh and rather innocent quality he detected in Maggie Trent alongside the expensive grooming and the stunning green eyes?

He shook his head, mainly to dislodge an image of her without her clothes—she was David Trent's daughter, after all—and reminded himself that she could certainly stand up for herself.

But that produced another inclination in him. As well as speculating on her figure, he discovered a desire to indulge in more verbal fencing with her.

Hell, Jack, he thought, isn't that a little immature? Not to mention a dead-end street with this particular girl?

In the meantime, Maggie discovered she was clutching her mobile phone as tightly as if she wished to crush it, so she put it, together with her notes, carefully on the roof of her car and planted her hands on her hips as she delivered her reply.

'At this moment, yes to all of those names, Mr McKinnon,' she said through her teeth. 'But since I'm here at the express instructions of the owner in my capacity as a real-estate agent, you *can't* be here legitimately so would you mind moving on?'

He smiled fleetingly, thought, Immature? Maybe, but what do they say? Men will be men! And he took his time about summing her up from head to toe again.

With a rural inspection to do, Maggie wore jeans, short boots and a pink blouse. Her hair was fishplaited and she wore the minimum of make-up, only lip gloss, in fact. It was also her last assignment of the day so she'd gone home to change into something suitable for tramping round a paddock.

None of that hid the fact that she was long-legged, high-breasted and had a particularly lithe way of walking that was an invitation to imagine that supple, golden body in your arms, in your bed…

Nor, he noted, did his scrutiny of her breasts, hips and legs, her smooth, silky skin, indeed his systematic stripping of her, go unnoticed.

Once again, bright colour flooded her cheeks, but at the same time her eyes started to sparkle with rage.

He observed the wrathful turmoil he was exciting in her with another smile, this time dry.

'So that's what you do for a—shall we say hobby? But it so happens you're wrong, Miss Trent,' he said. 'I was also contacted by the owners. They want to know if this property has development potential.'

Maggie closed her eyes in sheer frustration. 'They didn't say a word about that to me!'

He shrugged. 'You're welcome to check back with them.'

She reached for her phone, but put it down on the roof of her car again as her emotions ran away with her. 'You can't—you wouldn't! It's so lovely. It would be a crying shame.'

'To destroy it and cover it with little boxes?' he suggested, and strolled into the shed.

Maggie followed him. 'Yes!'

'Listen.' he turned on his heel towards her and she nearly ran into him. 'A lot of you do-gooders amaze me.'

She backed away a step.

It was impossible not to be slightly intimidated by Jack McKinnon. He was tall, for one thing, and he moved with superb co-ordination. His grey gaze was boring right into her and the lines and angles of his face were set arrogantly beneath that dark fair hair. The arrogance was compounded by a beaky nose and a well-cut but hard mouth and—at such close quarters there was even more to contend with.

He was so essentially masculine it was impossible to be in his company without a sense of man versus woman coming into the equation.

That translated, she realized, to a competitive form of self-awareness that took her by surprise. An 'I can be just as judgmental of you, Jack McKinnon, because I can be just as alluring, sexy and damned attractive as—as Lia and Bridget are!'

She blinked as it shot through her mind. Could she? She doubted it. She had never mentally stripped a man the way he had stripped her and she was quite sure she couldn't render him as hot and bothered—and stirred up, she acknowledged honestly—as his lazy, sensual summing-up of her had. Not to mention—how dared he do that to her? Who did he think he was?

There was also, if all that weren't bad enough—and she wondered why she hadn't taken this into account before because even her mother had mentioned it!—the distinct impression that he was diabolically clever, as he proceeded to demonstrate.

'If you have real concerns about the environment and the impact of urban sprawl, take them to the city council. If you object to rural zonings being over-turned do something positive about it,' he said contemptuously.

'Something?' she echoed unwisely.

'Yes. Campaign against it. Stand for council yourself. Use your ballot power to vote for a 'greener' council. It can be done. But don't rail against me in a virtually uneducated fashion, because I'm not breaking any laws at all.'

'What about moral and philosophical laws?' she challenged. 'What about enriching yourself at the expense of the environment and people like the Smiths?'

'I have no idea who the Smiths are but...' he paused and once again that grey gaze roamed over her, although this time clinically and coldly '...it's often the wealthy, the old money entrenched in their ivory towers and open green spaces, who lack concern and understanding for the less fortunate majority of the population.'

Maggie gasped. 'That's not true, of me anyway!'

'No?' He raised a sardonic eyebrow. 'You should try being one of that majority, Miss Trent. You should experiment with existing as a couple and raising a family on a single income because the kids are too small to leave, or child-care is too expensive—and see what it means to you to have your own roof over your head.'

'I—'

But he continued scathingly, 'You may think they're little boxes, but they're *affordable* and they're part of the great Australian dream, owning your own home. Come to that, it's a vast continent but inhospitable, so suburbia and the fact that we cling to the coast is another fact of life.'

He paused and eyed her. 'How much does your privileged background stop you from understanding some basic facts of life?' he asked her then. 'How many acres does your father own all green, untouched and lovely?'

That was when Maggie completely lost her temper. One innuendo, one insult too many, she raged inwardly, and looked around for some way to relieve the pressure of it all—she grabbed the door and banged it closed.

'I hope,' he said as the echoes of it slammed around the shed, 'this isn't what I think it is.'

'And I hope it demonstrates to you the force of my emotions about the likes of you,' she returned icily.

He looked around with a gathering frown and mentally castigated himself for playing verbal war games with this girl. 'Are your emotions savage enough to want to kidnap me?'

'Savage enough to make me want to scream and shout, throw things and slam things—' Maggie stopped abruptly. 'Kidnap you? What on earth are you talking about? The last thing—'

'One wonders if your antipathy is towards my housing estates or the kind of man you think I am?' His grey glance brushed over her insolently. 'So you have a key in your pocket?'

Maggie looked bewildered. 'What do you mean? A key? No. Why?'

He walked past her to the closed shed door and turned the handle. Nothing happened. 'This door is now deadlocked. From memory, you had a key in this lock but on the outside, didn't you?'

'Yes.' Maggie stopped and her lips parted as understanding of what she'd done started to seep through. 'Yes.' She cleared her throat. 'But there must be other ways out.'

'Show me,' he commanded. 'As far as I can see the only two windows have burglar bars fitted and both doors are locked now.'

'Oh, my…' Maggie breathed. 'I don't believe this! What about your keys? You must have had some.'

'No. I wasn't really interested in the house or the shed.'

'Well, well—phones,' she gabbled, and was hit by the memory of her mobile sitting on the roof of her car. She closed her eyes. 'Please tell me you've got your mobile phone on you?' she begged.

'I don't. I left it on its mounting in my car. This is all very affecting, Ms Trent,' he said with utter contempt, 'but whatever you *don't* like to call it, and for whatever reason you decided to deprive me of my liberty—' his gaze was cold enough to slice right through her '—you're going to pay for this.'

'Hang on, hang on.' Maggie took some deep breaths. 'It was an accident. Yes, OK, maybe I got a bit carried away, but I have every right to, on the Smiths' behalf if nothing else! There is no reason in the world, however,' she said emphatically, 'that would make me want to kidnap you!'

'The ubiquitous Smiths again,' he murmured, then said trenchantly, 'Lady, you were bestowing enough attention on me last Sunday to make the hairs on the back of my neck stand up.'

Maggie sucked in her cheeks in the effort she made not to blush. 'That was the power of my disapproval,' she offered stiffly.

'Oh, yeah?' He said it softly, but the two words contained a world of disbelief.

'Yes!' she insisted at the same time as a most treacherous little thought slipped into her mind— So why hadn't she been the same since?

But that spurred her on to say hotly. 'You can't

have it both ways, Mr McKinnon. Either I'm a man-hater or I'm not!'

He lifted an eyebrow. 'Perhaps I should qualify that—a hater of wealthy, powerful men completely in love with themselves.'

'Bingo! Now you've got it right.'

'I wonder,' he mused. 'There could be two sides to that coin, but anyway—' he looked briefly amused '—I don't agree that I'm in love with myself so you mightn't have to hate me totally, or the opposite,' he added softly.

Maggie stared at him. 'I have no idea what you're talking about!'

He rubbed his chin and narrowed his eyes.

'Look…' She hesitated as she tried to gather her thoughts, then she threw up her hands. 'If I'd *lured* you here then locked you in, that would be a different matter, but it's a supreme coincidence the two of us being here today!'

'You could be a quick thinker for all I know,' he countered. 'And there are women who take the most amazing liberties and—opportunities.'

She studied the harsh lines of his face. She thought of the pent-up dynamism she'd sensed in him. She had to acknowledge that he would be extremely attractive to most women and when you added his wealth to his looks and his aura, you had also to acknowledge there could be some women, gold-diggers, fortune-hunters, who would take what opportunities they could.

'You forget,' she said quietly, 'I probably have as much money in my own right as you do.'

He said, with a flash of irritation, as if he was suddenly heartily sick of her, 'I don't really give a damn for your motivation. I'd much rather you worked out how to get us out of here. I have a plane to catch in a couple of hours.'

Maggie looked around helplessly, then upwards. 'Maybe—maybe we can go through the roof?'

He swore comprehensively and pointed out just how high the roof was and that there was no ceiling. There was also no sign of so much as a set of steps, let alone a decent ladder, or…

Maggie finally stemmed the tide. She planted her hands on her hips again. 'You're a man, aren't you? Surely you can think of something?'

He folded his arms and looked sardonic. 'Even wealthy, powerful men have their uses? Isn't that a double standard?'

Maggie opened and closed her mouth a couple of times.

'Cat got your tongue, Miss Trent?' he drawled. 'Never mind, here's what I suggest. Since you got us into this—*you* get us out.'

CHAPTER TWO

'THAT'S...that's ridiculous,' Maggie stammered.

'Why?'

'I thought you had a plane to catch.'

'I get the feeling even my best efforts won't catch me that plane.'

She gazed around in serious alarm. 'That doesn't entitle you to twiddle your thumbs!'

He looked her over sardonically, but she was entirely unprepared for what he said next.

'Let's try and clear the decks here. If you're not trying to make some stupid statement about the kind of housing estates I develop, what are you after, Maggie Trent? My body?'

She went scarlet, instantly and—it felt—all over, and could have killed herself. 'In your dreams, mister,' she said through her teeth.

'Why so hot, then?' he taunted and ran his gaze up and down her. 'We might suit rather well. In bed.'

Her tongue seemed to tie itself in knots as all her mental sensors seemed to attune themselves to this proposition in the form of a picture in her mind's eye of just that—Jack McKinnon running his hands over her naked body.

What was particularly surprising about it was the fact that she didn't often fantasize about men. In fact she'd sometimes wondered if there was something wrong with her. The other surprise she got was the realization that this man had got under her skin from the very beginning in this very way, and succeeded in unsettling her even when she'd been telling herself she hoped never to lay eyes on him again.

Perhaps, but that didn't mean she had to like it, or him, she thought.

'Look—' she ignored his assessing gaze; she ignored her burning cheeks '—don't push me any further with this kind of—cheap rubbish!'

He smiled slightly as he took in the imperious tilt of her chin. 'Ever tried a real man, Maggie, as opposed to a good-mannered, docile boy like Tim Mitchell?'

Her lips parted.

'You might find your stance on men somewhat changed if you did,' he drawled, and went on before she could draw breath. 'And if you're not making a statement on housing estates, what's left?'

'You tell me,' she suggested dangerously.

This time he smiled quite charmingly, although it didn't take the sting out of what he said. 'A flighty, spoilt little rich bitch who hates not getting her own way?' he mused. 'A right chip off the old block,' he added with that lethal smile disappearing to be replaced by a cold, hard glance of contempt. Then he turned away.

'Hang on! What's that supposed to mean? Do you…do you know my father?' she demanded.

He turned back casually. 'Everyone knows about your father. His high-handed reputation precedes him by a country mile.'

Maggie bit her lip, but she soldiered on. 'I told you—well, no, Tim told you, but all the same—I don't trade on my father.'

'Your kind generally stick together in the long run,' he observed and shrugged his wide shoulders.

'What "kind", exactly, is that?' she queried with awful forbearance.

He looked at her indifferently. 'Old money, class, breeding—whatever you like to call it.'

'People who make those kinds of statements generally have none of those advantages—but wish they did,' she shot back.

He grinned. 'You're right about one thing, I have no breeding or class, but you're wrong about the other—I have no desire to acquire them. Well, now that we've thoroughly dissected each other, not to mention insulted each other, should we get down to brass tacks?'

'And what might they be?'

'How to get out of here. Is anyone expecting to see you this afternoon or this evening? Does anyone know you're here?'

Maggie pulled out a chair and sat down at the table at the same time as, with an effort, she withdrew her mind from the indignity of being tarred with the same brush as her father again or, if not that, being classed as a flighty little rich bitch.

That one really stung, she discovered. True, she could be hot-tempered, as she'd so disastrously demonstrated, but it had no connection with being spoilt or rich. How to make Jack McKinnon see it that way—she shot him a fiery little glance—was another matter. Then again, why should she even bother?

She frowned and addressed herself to his question. 'The office knew I was going to do a property valuation, but I wasn't planning to go back to work this afternoon so they won't miss me until tomorrow morning, oh, damn,' she said hollowly.

He raised an eyebrow at her.

'I've just remembered. I wasn't planning to go into the office at all tomorrow.'

'Why not?'

'I have a doctor's appointment in the morning and I was going to spend the afternoon—' She broke off and grimaced a shade embarrassedly.

'Let me guess,' he murmured. 'Getting your hair done, a facial, a manicure, a dress fitting, perhaps a little shopping in the afternoon?'

Maggie's cheeks started to burn because most of the things he'd suggested were on her agenda for tomorrow afternoon. But she ignored her hot cheeks and beamed him a scathing green glance.

'Listen,' she said tersely, 'yes, my hours can be elastic. On the other hand sometimes they're extremely long and I have a day off this week, two actually, because I'm working *all* next weekend. I do not have any more time off than anyone else in the office!'

He shrugged.

Prompting her to continue angrily, 'And if I'm the only woman you know who gets her hair cut now and then, has a manicure occasionally and shops from time to time, you must mix with some strange types, Mr McKinnon.'

He studied her hair and her nails. 'They look fine to me,' he said smoothly, but with an ironic little glint. 'Be that as it may, only your doctor and your beautician are likely to miss you tomorrow I take it?'

Maggie sat back with her expression a mixture of frustration and ire. 'Yes!'

'Anything serious with the doctor?'

'No.'

'So they're hardly likely to mount a search and rescue mission.'

'Hardly.'

'You live alone?'

'I live alone,' she agreed. 'How about you?'

'Yep.'

'What about this plane you're supposed to catch?'

He looked thoughtful. 'It could be a day or two before I'm missed. I'm—I was—on my way to a conference in Melbourne, but I planned to call in on my mother tomorrow in Sydney on the way.'

Maggie sat up. 'Surely she'll miss you?'

'She didn't know I was coming. It was to be a surprise.'

'That's asking for trouble!' Maggie said. 'You could have missed *her*.'

'Apart from complicating our situation?' He waited until she looked slightly embarrassed. Then he added, 'Not much chance of missing her as she's not fit enough to go out.'

This time Maggie looked mortified. 'I beg your pardon,' she said stiffly.

His lips twisted. 'As it happens I'm in agreement with your first sentiment.'

She looked startled. 'Why?'

'I'm sorry now I didn't let her know, but the reason I don't usually is because if I don't turn up exactly at the appointed time, she gets all anxious and unsettled.'

'Oh.' Maggie found she had to smile. 'My mother's a bit like that.'

They said nothing for a few moments, both locked

into their thoughts about their respective mothers, then he shrugged and strolled over to the pile of tarpaulins in the corner and started to pull them off.

Maggie confidently expected an old utility vehicle or tractor to be revealed, so she sucked in an incredulous breath when a shiny black vintage car in superb condition and a Harley Davidson motor bike, both worth a small fortune, were exposed.

'They didn't—the owners didn't say a word about these!'

'No? It does explain the security, however,' he said. 'This shed is like a fortress.'

Maggie frowned. 'It doesn't make sense. They haven't lived here for over a year, they told me. They don't have a caretaker. The house is a shambles but, well, who in their right minds would—sort of—abandon these?' She got up and walked over to the car and stroked the bonnet.

'You would have thought they'd put them up on blocks at least,' Jack said. He opened the car door and they both looked in.

The interior was as beautifully restored as the rest of it with plump, gleaming leather seats and the keys were dangling in the ignition. Jack slid into the driver's seat and switched it on. The motor purred to life.

He let it run for a few minutes, then switched it off and got out of the car. 'They must know they're here,' he said. 'Someone has to be starting this car regularly or the battery would be flat.'

'What did they say to you?' she asked. 'The owners.'

'I didn't speak to them, but...' he paused '...same as you; they gave my PA to understand that no one had lived here for over a year. They certainly didn't mention any vintage cars and bikes to her, but I wasn't planning to come into the shed so...' He stopped.

Maggie turned on her heel and ran across to the kitchen cupboard. 'These tins,' she said, pulling out a can of baked beans, 'don't look over a year old. Nor—' she reached for an open packet of cornflakes and peered inside '—would these have survived the mice I happen to know are here. But they're fine.'

She proffered the packet to him.

He didn't look inside. 'I believe you. Are you saying someone has taken over this shed?'

'It's quite possible! The nearest neighbours are miles away on a different road. The driveway in here is virtually concealed. You could come and go and no one would be any the wiser!'

'If it's true it's not much help to us unless they actually live here and come home every night.'

'Maybe they do!' Maggie said with a tinge of excitement.

He walked round the car and opened the boot. 'Well, that's something, in case they don't.'

'What?' She went to have a look.

'A tool kit.' He hefted a wooden box out of the boot, put it on the floor and opened it. 'Of sorts,' he added and lifted out an electric key saw. 'We may just be able to cut our way out of here somehow.'

Maggie heaved a huge sigh of relief. 'Oh, thank heavens!'

He glanced across at her. 'Hear, hear.'

'In time to catch your plane?'

'No. This is more a hobby saw; it's going to be a long, slow process.'

'Why don't you get straight to work?' she suggested. 'I'll make us a cup of tea.'

The look he tossed her was full of irony.

'I've never used one of those,' she said, 'but if you'd like to show me how, you could make the tea and I could do the sawing. Would you prefer that?' she queried innocently.

'No, I would not. We could be here for a year,' he returned shortly.

Maggie hid a smile.

'But what you could do is scout around for an extension cord. The nearest power point is too far from the door—' He stopped abruptly and looked frustrated.

'There's power!' she assured him. 'And water. I checked.'

He looked relieved this time, but in no better humour. 'OK. Start looking for a cord.'

Maggie resisted the temptation to salute and say, Yes, sir! And she toned down her triumph when she found an extension cord on top of the kitchen cupboard.

An hour later, his mood was even worse. There were no spare blades for the saw and the one in it was blunt.

'This thing wouldn't cut butter,' he said, having succeeded in cutting no more than a shallow, six-inch-long groove in the door. He threw it aside in disgust.

It was dark by now and the only light was from a single bulb suspended from the rafters. Its thin glow didn't reach the corners of the shed, and the mice, having decided they weren't under threat from the humans who had invaded their space, were on the move again.

Maggie had made tea an hour ago, then coffee a few minutes previously. She now stared down into the dark depths of her cup, and shivered. 'We're not going to get out of here tonight, are we?'

He came over to the table and pulled out a chair. 'No, Miss Trent, we are not. Not unless whoever is moonlighting in this shed comes home.'

'So you agree someone *is* doing that?'

'Was there power connected to the house?'

Maggie thought swiftly. 'No. That's strange, isn't it? On here but not up there.'

'Whoever they are, they may have found a way to tap into the grid illegally.' He suddenly slammed his fist onto the table in a gesture of frustration.

'I...' she looked at him fleetingly '...I do apologize.'

'So you bloody well should.'

He had wood shavings in his hair and he brushed them off his shirt. There were streaks of dust on his trousers.

'You don't have to swear.'

'Yes, I do,' he contradicted. He looked at his hands. They were filthy and several knuckles were grazed. 'Would you like to know what I'd be doing now if I wasn't incarcerated here? I'll tell you.'

He glanced at his watch. 'I'd just be arriving at my hotel in Sydney where I'd shout myself a sundowner and have a shower. Then I'd order a medium-rare pepper steak with Idaho potatoes, maybe some rock oysters to start with and a cheese platter to follow. I feel sure I'd wash it all down with...' he stared at her reflectively '…a couple of glasses of a decent red, then maybe some Blue Mountain coffee.'

Maggie flinched inwardly and couldn't think of a thing to say.

'How about you?' he queried.

She thought for a moment. 'Toasted cheese with a salad and an early night,' she said briefly.

He lifted an eyebrow. 'That sounds very bachelor girl.'

'I am a bachelor girl.'

'A very well-heeled one by the same token,' he murmured.

Maggie started to feel less embarrassed and guilty. 'Don't start on all that again,' she warned.

'Why shouldn't I? If you were an ordinary girl rather than ultra-privileged, and if you were without strong, unreasonable prejudices, I wouldn't be here.'

'Listen, mate, you offered the first insult!'

'Ah, yes, so I did.' He grinned reminiscently. 'I take nothing back.'

'Neither do I. But you,' she accused, 'went on doing it.'

He shrugged. 'You have to admit it was a rather bizarre situation to find myself in.'

Maggie frowned. 'What did you mean there being two sides to that coin? The one about me hating powerful, arrogant men or words to that effect?'

'Sometimes,' he said reflectively, 'girls are secretly attracted to power and arrogance in men even if they don't like to admit it.'

'I am not one of those, assuming they exist and are not a figment of your imagination,' Maggie stated.

He grinned. 'Very well, ma'am. And it doesn't

make you at all nervous to be locked in here with me in our current state of discord?'

Maggie hesitated. 'I know it must have looked rather strange, what I did,' she said slowly, 'and I suppose I can't blame you for wondering what on earth was going on. Therefore everything you said, even although I found it offensive—'

'All that cheap rubbish?' he interrupted gravely, although with an inward grin.

'Yes.' She eyed him briefly and sternly. 'Therefore everything you said was—understandable, perhaps, so—'

'I see.'

'Will you stop interrupting?' she commanded. 'This is hard enough as it is.'

'My lips are sealed,' he murmured.

She eyed him dangerously this time. 'Put plainly, I'd much rather you disliked me and were irritated by me than any other ideas you might have had, all the same!'

He laughed softly, then he watched her intently for a long moment. 'Are you really that naïve, Maggie Trent?'

'What's naïve about it? Well,' she hastened to say, 'perhaps I am, in a general sense. I did have a very sheltered—' She broke off and bit her lip.

'Upbringing?' he suggested.

'My father—' She stopped again. She might have her problems with her father—she did!—but broadcasting them to strangers was another matter.

'Saw to that, did he?' Jack McKinnon eyed her reflectively. 'I'm surprised he let you out of his sight.'

Maggie drew a deep breath, but discovered she couldn't let this go. 'The fact that I actually have a job and live on my own is testimony to a battle for independence that you might find quite surprising.'

He said nothing, but the way he stared at her led her to believe he might be reviewing all the facts he now had at his disposal, and changing his opinions somewhat. Good, she thought, and, with a toss of her head, stood up.

She would have died if she'd known that he was actually contemplating the—pleasure?—yes, of having her as his dinner companion at his mythical dinner in Sydney, then disposing of her clothes article by article in a way that drove her wild with desire even if she didn't like him particularly...

'You know,' she said blandly, 'it's just occurred to me that I could alleviate at least one of your discomforts.'

He looked supremely quizzical. 'You could?' And wondered what she'd say if he told her at least one of his discomforts sprang from the way he kept thinking how she'd look without her clothes...

She went over and rummaged in the kitchen cupboard. What she produced was half a bottle of Scotch. She gathered two glasses and a jug from below the sink. She rinsed them all out, filled the jug with water and placed everything on the table.

'It may be tinned food rather than steak, oysters and cheese but at least we can have a drink—we may even find it puts us in a better mood.'

He studied her offerings, then studied her expression. 'Miss Trent, you are a peach.' He reached for the bottle.

She was right.

After a Scotch and a meal of a heated-up Fray

Bentos steak pie and baked beans, Jack McKinnon was rather more mellow.

'Tell me about the Smiths,' he said as she prepared to wash the dishes.

Maggie looked rueful and did so as she found a small bottle of dish detergent and squirted some green liquid into the sink. 'The thing is—' she turned on a tap '—is it ethical?'

'To offer people who hold out more money?' he mused. 'There's no law against it.'

Maggie eyed the mound of bubbles building in the sink. 'It's going to drive Sophie and Ernest mad for the rest of their lives.' She switched off the tap.

'Don't you think the heart of this dilemma might lie elsewhere?'

She turned to him. 'Elsewhere?'

'Such as…' he paused '…Ernest jumping at the chance to get out of a property he was finding too much for him—and even the original price was a very fair one, believe me—while Sophie wanted to stay? A marital lifestyle dilemma, in other words.'

Maggie started to wash the dishes in silence. 'Perhaps,' she said eventually.

'And did you know, Maggie, that I always exceed the town planning regulations regarding open spaces, sports fields and community centres like kindergartens? They may appear to you like little boxes, the houses I build, but they're always well provided with those facilities. And while my houses may not be mansions, they are not shonky.'

'I'll…I'll have to take your word for it, Jack.' She rinsed the last dish, then turned to face him. 'On the other hand, I could not but regret *this* property, for example, being scraped bare and built on.'

He was sitting back looking relaxed, even amused, although she wasn't sure why.

'What?' she asked with a frown.

'I'm in agreement with you, that's all.'

She blinked. 'But you said—'

'I said I was contacted about it with a view to urban development. As you probably know that would mean applying for a re-zoning that I doubt I'd get, but that's not why I came to look at it personally.'

'It isn't?'

He shook his head. 'I'm interested in providing a buffer zone now.' He ruffled his hair. 'So I'm looking for the right properties to provide it. I'm also looking for one that I might live on. This could be it.'

Maggie stared at him with her mouth open and all sorts of expressions chasing through her eyes.

'I felt sure the irony of that would appeal to you,' he drawled. 'Why don't you sit down and have another drink with me before you explode?'

'I…you…this…I will,' Maggie said. 'Of all the…' She couldn't find the words and she dropped into a chair and accepted the glass he handed her.

'Double standards?' he suggested.

'Yes! Well…'

He laughed softly. 'But at the same time preserving the rural environment? That is a tricky one.'

'I was thinking about you joining the "ivory tower" club after all you said on the subject,' she returned arctically.

'Oh, I don't think there's any chance of that,' he drawled.

Maggie sipped some Scotch gratefully. It was getting cold. As she felt the warmth of it go down she watched him covertly.

He had his hands shoved in his pockets, he was sprawled back and he appeared to be lost in thought.

It suddenly struck Maggie with a peculiar little pang that Jack McKinnon was actually in a class of his own. Much as she would like to, she couldn't deny his ivory-tower-club theory, although she'd certainly fought her own battles against being drawn into the socialite/debutante kind of society he meant: the polo, the races, fashion shows, winter skiing/summer cruise followers.

She'd always longed for a broader canvas. She wanted to work; she wanted to travel, but a different circuit from the one her father and his friends travelled from one exclusive resort to another.

She wanted, she realized, to know people like this man and overcome his basic contempt for her kind. Yet, it struck her with some irony, only hours ago she'd been so angry with him, her thoughtless expression of it had reinforced everything he disliked about her 'kind'.

The mystery of it all, though, was why did it matter so much to her? There was a whole world of unusual, interesting people out there...

'So what do you suggest?'

She came out of her reverie at his question to find him watching her narrowly, as if he'd got the vibes that her preoccupation was to do with him, and she moved a little uncomfortably.

'Uh—what do you mean?'

He shot her a last lingering look, then got up and stretched. 'Where do we sleep, Miss Trent?'

'That's not a problem. I've already worked it out,' she told him as her mind moved like lightning. 'I'll use the back seat of the car. You can—' she gestured '—use the settee.'

He grimaced. 'Quick thinking, that.'

'You're too long for the car,' she pointed out reasonably.

'I'm too long for the settee and it looks filthy.' He crossed over and tested it, then looked down at it critically. 'On the other hand, if this is what I think it is,' he said slowly, 'I might not be so hardly done by after all.'

'What do you mean?'

He pulled off the cushion seats, pulled up a bar and the settee converted itself into a sofa bed. What was more, it was made up with fairly clean-looking sheets, a thin blanket and two flat pillows.

'Diagonally, I might just fit if I bend my knees.'

'Lucky you,' she said rather tartly.

He cocked his head at her. 'While you're left without a blanket or any covering—is that what you're suggesting?'

She shrugged.

'The penalty for such quick thinking,' he murmured, and laughed at her expression. 'Here's what we'll do. Did you happen to see a pair of scissors in the kitchen cupboards or drawers?'

Maggie went to check and came back with a rusty pair. 'Only these.'

'They'll do.'

'What are you going to do?'

'This. Not our property obviously, but desperate circumstances call for desperate measures and we can replace them.'

He made several cuts then, using both hands, he ripped the double blanket and two sheets in half. He handed her hers ceremonially along with one of the pillows. 'There you go. I may never belong to the ivory tower club, but I can be a gentleman of sorts.'

She knew from the wicked look in his grey eyes that the joke was on her, but not what the joke was. She suspected it could be more than the ivory tower club, but…?

'Don't worry about it, Maggie Trent,' he said softly, but with more humour apparent in his eyes. 'Go to bed.'

Maggie turned away slowly. Before she did go to bed, she removed her boots, released her hair and paid a visit to the bathroom. Then she climbed into the back seat of the car, only to climb out again.

'What?' He was seated on the sofa bed taking his shoes off.

'I think it would be a good idea to leave the light on.' She gestured widely. 'Might deter the mice from getting too friendly.'

'You're scared of mice?'

'Not *scared*,' she denied. 'I just don't like the idea of close contact with them. Do you?'

'Not particularly. OK. It can stay on.'

'Thank you.' She hesitated as she was struck by an amazing thought—that her arbitrary organization of the sleeping choices might have been a miscalculation. Or, put it this way, she would feel much safer and more comfortable if she were to share the sofa bed with him, purely platonically of course.

Her eyes widened as she combed her fingers through her hair and posed a question to herself— You're not serious?

'Maggie?'

'Uh—' some colour came to her cheeks '—noth-

ing. It's nothing. Goodnight,' she said and could have
shot herself for sounding uncertain.

'Sure?'

'Mmm…' She marched over to the car and got in
again.

Jack McKinnon waited until she'd closed the door,
wound down a window and disappeared from view.
Then he lay back, pulled his half of the thin blanket
up and examined his very mixed feelings on the subject of Maggie Trent.

Something of a firebrand, undoubtedly, he wouldn't
be here otherwise—he grimaced. Plenty of hauteur,
as well, a good dose of her father's genes, in other
words, yet her personality was curiously appealing in
a way her father's could never be, not to him anyway.

How so? he asked himself. She'd exhibited just
about every failing you might expect from a spoilt
little rich girl, even to ordering him to sleep on the
sofa.

Perhaps it was the power of her emotions, then, he
mused. Even if misguidedly, she was passionate about
the environment. She felt deeply about the plight of
the Smiths—he grimaced again. But there was something else…

Her *peachiness*? That damned word again… OK,
then, she was lovely. About five feet four, he judged,
her figure was trim, almost slight, but he got the feeling it might be delightful: delicately curved, velvety
nipples, small, peachy hips—yes, the word did fit
somewhere!—satiny skin and all that tawny hair, not
to mention stunning eyes to set it off. But what was
it that puzzled him about her—an aura of sensual un-
awareness?

Maybe, he thought, then amended the thought to—

sometimes… When he'd mentally stripped her she'd got all hot and bothered as well as angry. Now, though, being trapped in a shed with a strange man, virtually, who *had* mentally stripped her, appeared not to faze her. Why not?

Had a habit of command kicked in that didn't allow her even to contemplate things getting out of hand? Whatever, he concluded with an inward smile, it was rather intriguing and refreshing. Not that he'd do anything about it…

So why—he posed the question to himself—was he not more…absolutely furious about the current state of affairs? True, he'd been frustrated and irritable when trying to saw through the door, he'd been incredulous and angry when it had first happened, but…

He shrugged. All the same, he was going to have to come up with something tomorrow. He stared upwards. If he could figure out a way to get up to the roof, that might be his best shot after all.

Maggie arranged herself as best she could on the back seat of the car, only to discover that sleep suddenly seemed to be the furthest thing from her mind.

She was confused, she realized. Confused, tense and annoyed with herself. What an incredibly stupid thing to do! Would she ever grow out of these rash, hot-headed impulses that plagued her from time to time? When *would* they get out of this wretched shed?

Well, that explained the tension and the annoyance, she reasoned, but what was she confused about?

Jack McKinnon, it came to her. It seemed to be impossible to tear her thoughts away from him! Because she didn't understand him? Was that so surprising? She barely knew him, but, going on what she did know of him, his reactions *had* been rather surprising.

Yes, there was still that underlying contempt, there had been open contempt, but he *could* have made things much more uncomfortable for her. He could have treated her far more severely and scathingly... Had she misjudged him? Well, no, he had offered the first insult. Then again, that had obviously been based on her father's reputation.

All the same, she hadn't expected to end up liking him...

She sighed exasperatedly and closed her eyes.

Jack woke up at three o'clock.

As he glanced at his watch he was amazed that he'd slept so long; he didn't need much sleep. What also amazed him was the sight of Maggie Trent asleep at the table with her head pillowed on her arms.

He sat up abruptly and the rusty springs of the sofa bed squeaked in protest.

Maggie started up, wide-eyed and alarmed. 'Who...what...?'

'Only me,' he said reassuringly. 'What's the matter?'

'I...just couldn't sleep. It was like being in a coffin, no, a hearse,' she corrected herself. 'I felt seriously claustrophobic.'

'You should have told me earlier!'

She eyed him, then smiled, a faint little smile of pure self-mockery. 'I do sometimes find it hard to admit I could be wrong about—things.'

He grimaced, then had to laugh. 'OK.' He got up. 'That admission earns you a spell on the bed.'

'Oh, you definitely wouldn't fit into the car, so—'

'Don't argue, Maggie,' he ordered. 'I have no intention of trying the car anyway.'

'But it's only three o'clock,' she pointed out. 'What will you do?'

'Seriously apply myself to getting us out of here. Come on, do as you're told.'

Maggie got up reluctantly, but she sank down onto the sofa bed with a sigh of relief. Then she frowned. 'Does that mean you haven't been serious about getting us out of here until now?'

He glanced at her. Her hair was spread across the pillow and even in the feeble light her eyes were discernibly green—he couldn't remember knowing anyone with those colour eyes, he thought, then remembered her father. Of course. His mouth hardened.

'Let's just say I don't like being thwarted.' He turned away.

'Did that annoy you,' she asked, 'me saying you weren't serious?'

He shrugged. 'It reminded me that I've been in this damn shed for long enough.'

'You've been—for the most part—you've been pretty good about it. I do appreciate that.'

'Yes, well, why don't you go to sleep?'

She didn't answer immediately, then, 'The more I think about it, the roof is the only way to go. I hate to say I told you so, but if we could get up there somehow, it is only an old tin roof and maybe we could prise one of the sheets open or apart or something. I'm actually quite good at climbing.'

He was stretching and he turned to her with his arms above his head.

Maggie took a strange little breath as the full impact of his beautiful physique hit her.

'Climbing?' he said.

'I used to do gymnastics, seriously, and I've done an abseiling course. I'm not afraid of heights and I have good balance.' She looked upwards. 'I wouldn't have any trouble balancing on those beams.'

He studied her thoughtfully, then stared around. 'If I got onto the roof of the car and you got onto my shoulders, you might just reach a beam.'

Maggie sat up. 'Yes!' She subsided. 'But what to use to attack the roof with?' she asked whimsically.

The toolbox he'd got the saw out of was lying on the floor next to the table. He bent over and pulled out a short chrome bar. 'Heaven alone knows what this is for, but it might do, although—' he grimaced '—whether you'd have the strength—'

She cast aside the blanket and got up. 'I could try!'

He hesitated a moment longer, then shrugged. 'We'll give it a go.'

Five minutes later they were both on the roof of the car.

'Just as well they built them solidly in those days,' he commented with a fleeting grin, and squinted upwards. 'OK, here's what we'll do.'

He had both halves of the blanket. 'I'm going to try and throw these over the beam. That should give you something to work with. Look—' he stripped off his shirt '—take this up with you. Once you get up there, if you do, you'll need as much protection from splinters as you can get and I'll also tie the bar into one sleeve. You sit down while I throw.'

This time she did say it—'Yes, sir!'—but good-naturedly and even with something akin to excitement in her voice.

He looked down at her. 'You're a strange girl, Maggie Trent.'

'I know,' she agreed.

He opened his mouth as if to say more as they gazed at each other, but changed his mind.

Maggie sat down cross-legged and tied his shirt around her waist. It took him several attempts, but he finally got both bits of blanket dangling over the beam.

'Now for the tricky bit.' He knelt down. 'Climb onto my shoulders. Don't worry, I won't drop you and I won't fall myself—I also have good balance.'

'Are you a gymnast too?' Maggie asked.

'No, but I did some martial arts training in my misguided youth.'

Maggie climbed onto his shoulders. 'Well, I'm happy to know I wasn't completely wrong about you.'

'Oh?'

'I took you for a much more physical guy who'd prefer to be climbing Mount Everest rather than building housing estates.'

'Really.' He grinned. 'That should provide an interesting discussion at another time. Are you comfortable, Miss Trent? If at any stage you would rather not be doing this, for heaven's sake tell me. I won't hold it against you and we can all be wrong at times.'

Maggie looked down at the top of his head and placed her hands lightly upon it. 'Up you get—I was going to say Samson, but your hair's not long enough. I'm fine.'

'Here's hoping you don't have any Delilah tendencies,' he commented wryly and brought his hands up to wrap them around her waist. 'Here goes.'

He got to his feet slowly and steadily. At no time did Maggie feel insecure and at all times she had to appreciate his strength and co-ordination.

When he was upright, she carefully lifted her hands until she was able to grasp the blankets.

'All right?' he queried, his breath rasping in his throat.

'I've got them.' She tied the ends together and wrapped her hands in them. 'If I could stand up, I could reach the beam. It would be just above waist-height and easier to vault onto. I'd also have the blanket as a sort of safety strap.'

'Are you very sure, Maggie?'

'Yep. Can you handle it, though?'

'No problem. Easy does it.'

Putting her weight on the blankets, Maggie levered herself up onto her feet. 'I'm not hurting you, am I?' she asked anxiously as she felt his hands close round her ankles.

'What do you think I am?' he countered.

'Very strong. Well…' she swallowed '…here goes again.' A moment later as he rocked beneath her but stayed upright she was straddling the rafter.

'Well done, Maggie!'

She beamed down at him. 'Piece of cake. I did win a state title, you know.'

'I believe you. So. If you can crawl along it towards the wall, where the roof is at its lowest you could do a recce. Still got the bar?'

She untied his shirt from her waist and felt the sleeve. 'Yes. Yuck, it is full of splinters and nails, this beam, as well as cobwebs!'

'Be very careful.'

'Care is my middle name. Actually Leila is my middle name, after my grandmother—why am I babbling?' she asked at large as she started to crawl along the beam.

'Exhilaration? Stress? I don't mind. I don't have a middle name,' he said as he watched her inch her way forward.

'How come?' Maggie stopped moving and stared down at him.

He shrugged. 'I was adopted as a baby, although that may not have a thing to do with it.'

'You're joking!' she said incredulously. 'But you were talking about your mother!'

'She's my adoptive mother. Why am I babbling?' he asked humorously.

'Well, I'll be…' Maggie shook her head and started to inch forward again. 'Then you have done tremendously well for yourself! But it must have had some effect. Are you full of neuroses and so on?'

'Oh, definitely,' he said with a straight face, but a world of devilry in his eyes.

'I'm not sure I should believe that—ouch!'

'What?' he queried.

'A nail. I seem to have got my blouse hooked on it. Damn.' She struggled upright to the tune of tearing material as the front of her blouse ripped from the neckline to the waist.

'Take it off,' he suggested, 'and put my shirt on instead. The material might be tougher. Then use yours and a blanket to protect yourself.'

'Roger wilco!' She wrestled her blouse off, sitting easily enough on the beam with her feet hooked together beneath it. But just as she was about to put his shirt on they both froze at a loud noise outside the shed—a motor revving then being shut off followed by a car door slamming.

'Maggie, come down,' Jack said softly but urgently.

'Of course. We're about to be rescued!'

'Perhaps. But if this shed has been hijacked and there's something fishy going on, we may not be too welcome and I can't look after you up there.'

'OK, OK, I'm coming,' she whispered and backed along the beam until she was above him. 'Now!'

She slithered down the blankets and into his arms, leaving his shirt and her blouse dangling on the beam. At the same time the door was thrown open from the outside, a powerful searchlight was shone in and a string of expletives in a harsh male voice was uttered.

Maggie gasped and clutched Jack, completely dazzled by the light. He put his arms around her.

'Bloody hell!' the same harsh voice said. 'What is this—some sort of kinky sex set-up?' And to Maggie's utter disbelief the searchlight moved away revealing, not one, but two men, and some flash bulbs went off.

Jack growled in his throat, then he said into her ear, 'One, two, let's get down, Maggie.'

'OK,' she whispered back, and on his call of two they slithered down to the boot, then hit the floor together. He held her in his arms only until she was steady on her feet, then he strode forward to confront the two men.

Things happened so quickly after that, she couldn't believe her eyes. Both men backed away from him until one of them, the man with the camera, tripped and fell over a chair. He dropped the camera and Jack swooped onto it.

'I am sorry about this,' he said quite politely as he opened the back of it and exposed the film, 'but you wouldn't want to be responsible for some highly misleading pictures, now would you?'

The man got up nervously and dusted himself off. 'Not if you say so, mate,' he agreed.

'Good! Why don't you both sit down and tell me who you are? Sophie,' Jack added over his shoulder, 'you might be better off waiting in your car.'

It took a moment for Maggie to twig that he was talking to her, but as soon as she did she accepted the suggestion gratefully. It was still one of the hardest things she'd ever done—to achieve a dignified exit wearing only her socks, jeans and her bra. She did resist the temptation to run, however, until she was out of the shed, then she spurted to her car, climbed in with a sigh of sheer relief, and reached over into the back seat for the denim jacket she'd tossed there the day before.

It was fifteen minutes before Jack came out to her and he stopped on his way to retrieve his mobile phone and bag from his Range Rover and then to lock it.

He got into the passenger seat, glinted her a daredevil little smile and said, 'Home, James, I think.'

'What about your—?'

'Maggie, just go,' he commanded. 'I've done my level best to protect your fair name, let's not hang around.'

She switched the motor on and nosed the car forward. Two minutes later, she turned out of the concealed driveway onto the road and turned to him. 'I'm dying of curiosity! Who were they? What did you tell them? Do they still think we were…we were…?' She stopped and coloured painfully.

He was fishing around in his bag and he dragged a T-shirt out and shrugged into it with difficulty. 'Hang on,' he said as he began to punch numbers into his phone. 'What's your address?'

She told him.

It was someone called Maisie he rang—a Maisie who didn't object to being woken at four-thirty in the morning and given all sorts of instructions.

To wit, someone was to retrieve his Range Rover at the farm address, using his spare keys; someone was to pick him up at Maggie's address in about half an hour; a new flight to Melbourne was to be booked for him later in the day, no, he wouldn't be stopping in Sydney this time—what had happened to him?

'I was kidnapped by a girl, locked in a shed and—maybe I'll tell you the rest of it one day, Maisie, just be a love and sort all that out for me, pronto.'

He ended the call.

Maggie looked over at him. 'That's not funny!'

'No? I have to tell you it has been one of the funnier days of my life, Maggie Trent,' he said with his eyes glinting. His hair was standing up from his struggles with his T-shirt, and he ran his fingers through it.

She bit her lip and concentrated on her driving for a bit until he dropped his hand on her knee. 'All right. I apologize. Who were they? A private investigator and a journalist.'

Maggie's eyes widened. 'Oh, no!'

'As you say,' he agreed dryly, and told her the whole story.

The owners of the property had had a farm machinery hire business, now defunct. All the equipment had been stored in the shed, which explained why it was built like Fort Knox. They also had a wayward son, apparently, who'd stolen the vintage car and the bike on a whim and as a bit of a lark, and decided there was no better place to keep them under wraps than his parents' shed—he'd contrived to get copies of the keys made.

But he was also a garrulous young man when under the influence of liquor and drugs and the journalist, who wrote a motoring column and was a vintage-car freak himself, had got wind of the heist. He was also aware that the owner of the car and bike had hired a private investigator to look for them when the police had failed to trace them, so they'd decided to pool their resources.

'I see!' Maggie said at this point in the story.

'Yes,' Jack agreed. 'It all falls into place. How much more interesting to find Jack McKinnon and Margaret Leila Trent engaged in what could have looked like weird practices, though?'

She flinched. 'Do you think they believed our story? What did you tell them?' She pulled up at a traffic light on the Oxenford overpass.

'The truth, mostly. That the property was about to come onto the market and we were interested in it.'

'Perfectly true!'

'Yep.' He shot her an amused look. 'But I had to tamper with the truth a bit then. I told them the wind banged the shed door shut on us, locking us in.'

Maggie flinched again. 'That's a very small white lie,' she said, although uncertainly. 'Isn't it?'

'Almost miniature,' he agreed gravely. 'Uh—the light has changed, Maggie.'

She changed gear and moved forward a little jerkily. 'I know you're laughing at me,' she accused at the same time.

He did laugh outright then. 'Perhaps you should bear this incident in mind the next time you're moved to scream, shout and slam things,' he suggested and sobered suddenly. 'Because it wouldn't have been funny to be splashed across some newspaper because of who we are, *you* are particularly, and because it did look very strange.'

Maggie cruised to a stop at the next set of lights on the overpass. 'I never get these damn lights,' she said tautly, then sighed. 'You're right. I will.'

'Good girl. Anyway, I had to tell some more white lies. They think your name is Sophie Smith—'

'That was inspired,' she said gratefully and shivered suddenly.

He looked over at her and raised an eyebrow.

'I just thought of what my father would say if I got splashed across some newspaper in—those circumstances. He'd kill me! No, he wouldn't,' she corrected herself immediately, 'but he'd be furious!'

'He'd be more liable to want to kill me,' Jack said prosaically. 'However, although I suppose there always may be a question mark in their minds, those two have nothing to go on other than your car registration, and I don't think I gave them time to get it, in the dark.'

'It's not registered in my name. It's the firm's car,' she told him.

'Even better.'

'But—' she turned to him '—what about you? Do they know who you are?'

'They know and they're not likely to forget it.'

Maggie stared at him and shivered again. 'You can be very scary at times, you know.'

He shrugged. 'You've got a green light again, Maggie.'

She drove off. 'Not that I'm complaining,' she added. 'I'm very grateful to you for handling it all so well. Even my father would be grateful.'

'I wouldn't bet your bottom dollar on it.'

She drove in silence across Hope Island for a while, then as she turned into her street she said, 'What will we do now?'

He stirred. 'If I were you, Maggie, I'd go away for a while. Just in case they decide to snoop around a bit.'

'I can't just go away! I'm a working girl,' she objected, and pulled into her driveway.

Jack McKinnon looked through the window at her lovely villa and shrugged.

'Don't tell me we're back to all that nonsense!' she accused. 'What a spoilt little rich girl I am.'

His lips twisted as he transferred his gaze to her. 'Not entirely,' he said. 'Actually, I think you're one of a kind, Maggie Trent. On the other hand...' he paused and searched her eyes '...on the other hand you do bear some responsibility to your name and your family so it would be a good idea to take out some—' he gestured '—extra insurance. I'm sure that's what your father would advise and rightly so.'

He turned to look over the back of his seat as a car pulled up across the driveway. 'My lift has arrived.'

'Maisie?' she said.

'Not Maisie.'

'So…so that's it?' Her voice was slightly unsteady.

He grinned. 'A better outcome than it might have been, in more ways than one. You could still be balancing on a splintery beam trying to force open a tin roof.'

'Will you buy it? That property?'

'Don't know. Listen, you take care, Miss Trent.' He leaned forward and kissed her lightly, then he opened the door and slid out of the car, pulling his bag after him.

Maggie was still sitting exactly as he'd left her, with her fingers on her lips, when the other car drove off, taking Jack McKinnon out of her life.

Later in the day, a huge bouquet of flowers arrived for her with a simple message—'All's well that ends well, Jack.'

In the event, Maggie's mother was of exactly the same opinion as Jack McKinnon when she heard all about her daughter's ordeal. Not only did she insist that Maggie should go away for a while, taking a month's unpaid leave, but she also accompanied her for the first week.

CHAPTER THREE

THE ocean stretched forever beyond the arms of the bay. It was slate-blue and wrinkled. A layer of cloud rimmed the horizon, but the sun had risen above it and was pouring a path of tinsel light over the water. Long, lazy lines of swell were rolling in to crash onto the beach in a froth of sand patched white that looked like crazy paving until it slipped away.

To the south, the green, rock-fringed dome of Point Cartwright with its white observation tower stood guard over the mouth of the Mooloolah River.

To the north and much further away, the monolithic bulk of Mount Coolum stood out as well as Noosa Head, insubstantial in the distance. Closer to home Mudjimba Island lay in the bay like a beached whale complete with a tree or rock on its head to resemble a water spout. The whole area was known as the Sunshine Coast. It was an hour's drive north of Brisbane and it competed with the Gold Coast as a holiday destination.

Maggie withdrew her gaze from the distance and studied the beach. She was on the ninth floor of an apartment block in Mooloolaba, just across the road from it, a lovely beach, long and curved and protected from the dominant south-easterly trade winds. The road itself was lined with Norfolk pines, some as tall as the floor she was on.

There weren't many people on the beach although it was crisscrossed with footprints—the lull between

the serious early-morning walkers and the beach frol-
ickers.

It was an interesting spot, Mooloolaba. Its river was
home to a trawling fleet and wonderful fresh seafood
abounded. There were often huge container ships and
tankers anchored off Point Cartwright awaiting clear-
ance and pilots for their journey into Moreton Bay
and Brisbane, services that originated in Mooloolaba
together with an active Coastguard.

It was also a haven for many recreational mariners
on their voyages north or south. Mooloolaba was the
last stop before the Wide Bay bar, a treacherous wa-
terway between the mainland and Fraser Island, or the
first stop after it. Many a mariner had heaved a sigh
of relief to be safely inside the Mooloolah River after
a scary bar crossing and a sea-tossed trip south after
it. If you were sailing north, it was like a last frontier.

Is that what I'm facing? Maggie wondered suddenly. A last frontier...

She sat down at the small table and contemplated
her breakfast of fresh fruit and muesli, coffee and
croissants. She'd been in the luxury apartment for ten
days. It belonged to a friend of her mother's and had
no connection with the Trent name. Her mother had
spent the last week with her before having to go to
Sydney for a charity engagement she was unable to
break.

Her father, thankfully, was overseas on business
and she and her mother had agreed that he needn't
ever know about the episode in the shed.

She'd enjoyed the days with her mother—they'd
window-shopped, sunbathed, swum, walked, been to
the movies and read—but she was now bored and

ready to go back to work although she had two and half weeks of leave left, well…

She ate some muesli, then pushed the bowl away unfinished and poured her coffee. To be honest, she didn't know what she was ready for, but more of the same wasn't it and at the heart of the matter lay one man—Jack McKinnon.

She'd heard nothing more from him although she'd arranged to have her mail checked and all her phone calls rerouted to her mobile.

I wonder what he would think, she mused several times, if he knew how much I've changed my stance on him? If he knew I can't stop thinking about him, if he knew…come on, Maggie, be honest!…I seem to have fallen a little in love with him?

It was the strangest feeling, she reflected. While she'd been doing her 'trapeze act' she'd been a little nervous, but mostly fired with enthusiasm. She hadn't been aware of him as a man, only as a partner she could more than rely on. Now, the close contact with him invaded her dreams and made her go hot and cold in her waking hours when she thought about it.

Not only that, she might have felt annoyed by him at times—here she always paused and looked a bit guilty—but his company had *energized* her. It must have or why else would she be feeling as flat as a tack? Why else would she have this feeling she was at a last frontier in her life with nowhere she wanted to go?

Nor had her mother failed to notice her abstraction.

'Darling…' Belle regarded her seriously once '…did Jack McKinnon get you in just a little bit? Is that why you're so quiet sometimes?'

Maggie chose her words with care. 'If you have to get locked in a shed with a guy, he was all right.'

She got up abruptly, her coffee untasted. No good sitting around moping, she decided. Action was called for. She'd go for an invigorating swim.

The water was glorious. She swam out, caught a wave and surfed in expertly and she laughed at the sheer bliss of it as she lay on the sand with the water ebbing over her. That was when it came to her. If the mountain wouldn't come to her, she would go to it.

She packed her bags that morning and drove home.

Two days later, two very low-key days in case anyone was snooping about looking for her, she'd exhausted every avenue she could think of to get in touch with Jack McKinnon to no avail.

Either she was on a hit list of people to be kept away from him or he had the most zealous staff who kept *everyone* away from him. She couldn't even reach Maisie—no one seemed to have heard of a Maisie.

She'd even sat outside the headquarters of the McKinnon Corporation's head offices in her own car, not her firm's car, hiding behind dark glasses and a floppy linen hat, but she'd sighted neither the man himself nor his Range Rover.

She lay in bed that night, wide awake and with very mixed feelings as she listened to the mournful cries of the curlews on the golf course.

What had seemed so clear and simple to her in the surf at Mooloolaba was now assuming different proportions.

The polite spiels she got from a secretary saying

he was currently unavailable, but she'd be happy to take a message although she had no idea if, or when, Mr McKinnon would return it, were an embarrassment to her. Sitting outside his headquarters was the same—both were entirely out of character and she was finding it hard to live with the almost constant churning of her stomach and nervous tension involved.

Was she doing the right thing? It was all very well to tell herself that she didn't deserve to be brushed off like this, but if Jack McKinnon didn't want to be tracked down, should she respect his wishes?

Why, though? she asked herself passionately. Why was she such a *persona non grata* for him? Had she completely misread their, if nothing else, spirit of camaraderie in those last hours in the shed?

I guess, she thought forlornly, I really want an explanation from him, but that could be as embarrassing, if not to say as demoralizing, as what I'm going through now.

She turned over and punched her pillow, but still sleep didn't come. She got up and made herself a cup of tea. As she drank it and dawn started to rim the horizon it came to her that she would let it all drop. For one thing, she had no idea how to proceed now. For another, she wasn't feeling completely happy with herself.

She stared at the rim of light on the horizon and blinked away a sudden tear but when she went back to bed she slept until nine o'clock in the morning.

And it was a relief, although a sad one, the next morning, to have made the decision to stop her search.

Then her aunt Elena came to call, as she did fairly

regularly. Maggie invited her in and since it was that time of day asked her to stay to lunch—Elena was always good company.

She prepared open smoked salmon sandwiches drizzled with lemon juice and dusted with cracked pepper and she opened a bottle of chilled chardonnay to add to her lunch.

'How nice!' Elena approved.

'Let's sit outside,' Maggie suggested.

When they were comfortably installed on her terrace with a sail umbrella protecting them from the sun, they chatted about this and that until Elena said out of the blue, 'Your mother mentioned a while back that you'd met Jack McKinnon.'

Maggie went still and swallowed. 'What did she say?'

'That he was rather rude to you, so I'm thinking of taking him off my list of eligible bachelors.'

Maggie relaxed. Not that she had any qualms about Elena broadcasting the shed debacle, but she couldn't help feeling that the fewer people to know about it, the better. 'Oh, you don't have to do that on my behalf,' she said.

Elena settled herself more comfortably and sipped her wine. 'It's not only that, he's extremely elusive.'

Maggie eyed her humorously. 'That must be irritating for you.'

Elena grimaced. 'I've got *some* background on him. It's his love life that's the problem.'

Maggie hesitated, then she couldn't help herself. 'Background?'

Elena elucidated.

Jack McKinnon had been adopted as a baby by a loving but very average family. From an early age he'd exhibited above-average intelligence; he'd won scholarships to private schools and university, where he'd studied civil engineering and marine design.

Despite something of a mania for protecting his privacy, he appeared to be very normal considering his difficult start in life. He certainly wasn't ostentatious..no particularly fancy homes, no Lear Jets, et cetera.

'As for the women in his life—' Elena sighed '—he doesn't flaunt them and they don't talk once it's over.'

'What about…' Maggie thought briefly '…Lia Montalba and Bridget Pearson?'

'Both models, both Melbourne girls.' Elena frowned. 'I wouldn't class either of them as one of "his women". They were hired to advertise his catamarans. There's a big promotion coming out shortly, but both girls are back in Melbourne now.'

'Is there anyone at the moment?' Once again Maggie couldn't help herself.

'Not as far as I know. He does,' Elena said thoughtfully, 'have a hideaway. Maybe that's where he conducts his affairs.' She shrugged.

Maggie frowned. 'How do you know that?'

Elena tapped her nose. 'My sources are always classified, but he has a holiday home at Cape Gloucester—keep that to yourself please, Maggie! So, you reckon I should leave him on my list?'

'I…' Maggie paused as she tried to think straight. 'It doesn't matter one way or the other to me. Where…where is Cape Gloucester?'

'North Queensland. Up in the tropics near Bowen. I believe you have to drive through a cattle station to get to it, that's all I know.'

* * *

After Elena left, Maggie sat for a long time staring at the lengthening shadows on the golf course.

Was this fate? she wondered.

Everything she wanted to know including, perhaps, Jack's whereabouts, literally dropped into her lap?

Of course, she cautioned herself, he could also be in Sydney, New York or Kathmandu, but if he was at Cape Gloucester and she went up there, might that be the only way she would ever get the explanation she so badly wanted?

Working on the theory that what her mother didn't know about she couldn't worry about, Maggie left her a vague message and she packed her bags again and drove north. At least, she thought as she set off, she would be off the local scene, should a certain P.I. and journalist be looking for the mystery girl found in a shed in compromising circumstances with Jack McKinnon.

Or what might have looked like compromising circumstances, she reminded herself.

The Gloucester passage flowed between the mainland and Gloucester Island, a regal green island with several peaks. The passage, at the northern end of the Whitsunday Islands, was the gateway to Bowen and Edgecumbe Bay. It was a narrow strip of water and you could visualize the tide flowing swiftly through it. There were several sand banks and patches of reef guarded by markers.

It was remote and beautiful and, although you did have to drive through a cattle station to get to it, this was an improvement upon, until recent times, only being able to approach by sea.

There were two small beach resorts nestled into the tree-lined shores of the mainland, one overlooking Gloucester Island and Passage Islet, one overlooking Edgecumbe Bay. Maggie chose the one overlooking Gloucester Island; there was something about the island that intrigued her.

Her accommodation in a cabin was spacious and spotless and it was right on the beach. There was a coconut palm outside her veranda, there were casuarinas and poincianas, some laced with bougainvillea. Many of the trees had orchids growing from their bark; many of them were rather exotic natives like pandanus palms and Burdekin plums.

The coarse, dark crystals of the beach reminded Maggie of brown sugar, but the water lapping the beach was calm, crystal-clear and immensely inviting, especially at high tide. She spent an hour on her first evening sitting on the beach, watching fascinated as ripple after little silvery ripple raced along, tiny imitations of waves breaking on the beach.

Then she caught her breath in amazement as two strange ducks skimmed the water's edge—ducks that looked as if they were wearing leather yokes when in fact it was a strip of dark feathers on their creamy necks and chests. Burdekin Ducks, she was told, when she enquired.

There was only one other couple at the resort and she ate dinner with them before using a long drive as an excuse for an early night. In fact it was nervous tension making her yawn, she thought as she strolled back to her cabin. Had she done the right thing? Was he even here in his beach house tucked away amongst the trees beyond the resort? Why hadn't she gone to find out straight away?

'I'll be better in the morning,' she told herself. 'More composed. Less conscious of the fact that this is a man I'd pegged for the kind women rode off with into the sunset because they couldn't help themselves—and what's going to make me any different?'

She shook her head and went to bed.

The sun came up at six-fifteen. Maggie was walking along the beach at the time.

Gloucester Island was dark with its southern outline illuminated in gold; trees, beach and rocks were dark shapes pasted on a gold background as the sun hovered below the horizon. Then it emerged and light, landscape and seascape fell into place and fled away from her—and the tall figure walking along the beach towards her carrying a fishing rod was unmistakably Jack McKinnon.

Maggie took a great gulp of air into her lungs and forced herself to walk forward steadily, although he stopped abruptly.

When she was up to him she held out her hand. 'Dr Livingstone, I presume?'

He didn't reciprocate.

'OK, not funny—' Maggie dropped her hand '—but I nearly didn't find you, which brought to mind the Livingstone/Stanley connection, I guess. Are you not going to say anything?'

He took in her bare legs and feet, her white shorts, her candy-striped top and her pony-tail, and spoke at last. 'How did you find me?'

'That's classified. But if you were to offer me a cup of coffee, say, I'll tell you why I went to all the trouble I did.'

'Are you staying here?' He indicated the resort down the beach.

'Yep, although I've told no one why. Your secret is safe with me, Mr McKinnon.'

'Maggie,' he said roughly, then seemed to change tack. 'All right, since you've come this far the least I can do is a cup of coffee, I guess. Follow me.'

His house was only a five-minute walk away and from the beach you'd hardly know it was there. It was wooden, weathered to a silvery grey, two-storeyed, surrounded by trees and covered with creepers. A smart, fast-looking yacht under a tarpaulin was drawn up the beach on rails.

She followed him up the outside steps to the second storey and gasped at the view from his top veranda. Not only the Gloucester Passage lay before her, but also Edgecumbe Bay towards the mainland and Bowen, with its rim of mountains tinged with pink and soft blues as the sun got higher.

'You sure know how to pick a spot,' she said with genuine admiration. 'This is so beautiful.'

'It also used to be a lot further from the madding crowd before the road was opened,' he said.

'Including me?' She swung round to face him. 'What exactly is so maddening about me?' she asked tautly. 'Correct me if I'm wrong, but I thought a lot of our differences and misapprehensions about each other got sorted when we were trying to get out of the shed?'

He put the fishing line down and checked that the colourful lure with its three-pronged hook was tucked into a roundel on the rod out of harm's way. 'There are other differences you don't even know about, Maggie.'

He straightened and pushed his fingers through his hair. He wore khaki shorts and an old football Guernsey with the sleeves cut off above the elbows. He was brown, as if he'd spent quite a bit of time in the sun, and his hair was streaked lighter by it, and was longer, as if he'd forgotten to get it cut.

'If there are, why can't I know about them?' she countered. 'Believe me, I am not the spoilt little rich girl you mistake me for and I don't take kindly to being treated as such.'

His lips twisted and he folded his arms. 'So you don't think this exercise has labels stuck all over it shouting ''Maggie Trent has to get her own way''?'

Her nostrils flared. 'No. If anything it shouts, ''Maggie Trent deserves better''.'

'Better,' he repeated.

'Yes, better. As in—why on earth can't we get to know each other better? For example, I wouldn't dream of judging you on your father.' She stopped and bit her lip, then soldiered on, 'You know what I mean!'

'Men,' he said slowly, 'and their grievances don't always work that way.'

'Then perhaps you should take more notice of women,' Maggie suggested tartly. 'Come to that, the whole world might be a better place if people did.'

A reluctant smile chased across his mouth and he seemed about to say something, but he merely shrugged and walked inside.

Maggie hesitated, then she shrugged herself, and followed him.

*   *   *

His house was simple and open plan, but there was nothing rough and ready about it.

The floors were gleaming polished wood throughout. There was a low double bed covered with a faux mink throw and several European pillows covered in dusky pink linen. One bedside table was stacked with books, the other bore a beautiful beaten-copper lamp.

Two corner leather couches sat about a vast wooden coffee-table bearing more books and some model ships, one in a bottle. A big cabinet housed a television, stereo and DVD player. Brown wooden and raffia blade fans were suspended from the ceiling and louvre blinds protected the windows.

The kitchen was all wood and chrome and state-of-the-art with black marble bench tops. There were several cane baskets with flourishing indoor plants dotted about and on the wall facing the front door there was a huge, lovely painting of two gaudy elephants in soft greens, matt gold and dusky pink.

'Yes!' Maggie stared at it enchanted. 'The perfect touch.'

'Thank you.' He pulled a plunger coffee-pot out of a cupboard and switched on the kettle.

She watched him assemble ground coffee, mugs, sugar crystals and milk. 'Where did you get it?'

'What?'

'The painting?'

He glanced over his shoulder. 'Thailand.'

Maggie pulled a stool out from the breakfast bar and perched herself on it. 'Is there anything I can say to make this easier?'

'You don't appear to be having much difficulty as it is.' He spooned coffee grounds into the plunger and poured boiling water over them.

Maggie inhaled luxuriously. 'Believe me, never having done this before, I'm a basket case inside,' she said, however.

He stopped what he was doing and regarded her expressionlessly. 'Done what?'

She laced her fingers together on the counter. 'Well, changed my stance on a man rather drastically to begin with. Not,' she assured him, 'that I had much to do with that. It just—happened. Unfortunately there's a whole lot of baggage I carry that makes it—'

'You're talking about locking me in a shed first of all, then cornering me here?' he suggested dryly.

A hot sensation behind her eyes alerted Maggie to the fact that it would be quite easy to burst into tears of frustration—to her absolute mortification should she allow it to happen. It was obviously going to be much harder than she'd anticipated to get through to Jack McKinnon.

'It's not that I'm only after your body, nor do I have any agenda to do with forcing you round to my way of thinking on housing estates,' she said quietly.

He smiled with so much irony, she flinched. 'That's just as well,' he commented, and poured a mug of coffee and pushed it towards her. 'Because while *your* body is perfectly delightful, and has even deprived me of my sleep on the odd occasion, I don't intend to do anything about it.'

Maggie's eyes nearly fell out on stalks. 'Say that again!'

He hooked a stool towards him with his foot and sat down on the other side of the counter from her. 'You heard.'

'I may have heard, but it doesn't make sense.'

'No?' He shrugged and sipped his coffee. 'I thought if I removed the thorn from your flesh of me not appearing to return your physical interest, you might feel better about things. You might even go away.'

Maggie stared at him as he put his mug down. Then she stood up on a rung of her stool and slapped his face.

His coffee-mug overturned as he moved abruptly and a brown puddle stretched between them. Then the mug rolled off the counter in slow motion and smashed on the floor. It was the only sound although the thwack of her palm connecting with his cheek-bone seemed to linger on the air.

There was something utterly terrifying in the way his narrowed grey gaze captured hers as she sank back onto the stool; it was still and menacing and full of unconcealed contempt. It was also as impossible to tear her gaze away as it had been the day they'd first laid eyes on each other, until he moved again and snaked out a hand to capture her wrist.

Maggie panicked then. She tore her wrist away and slipped off the stool all set to run away as fast as she could. Two things impeded her: she slipped on the wet floor and yelped in pain. By the time she'd righted herself and realized she'd got a sliver of china in her foot, he'd come round the breakfast bar, grabbed her by the waist and lifted her into his arms.

Forgetting everything but the awful insult she'd received, she launched into speech. 'Yes, yes, yes!' she said, her green eyes blazing. 'Yes, OK, it has been a thorn in my flesh! I went from hating and despising you to liking you and—and—feeling as flat as a tack because all I meant to you was a *bunch of flowers*, obviously, but there's a singular difference between what you're implying and the facts of the matter—what are you *doing*?'

He strode over to a leather couch and sat down with her in his lap. 'This.'

Maggie struggled to free herself, but he resisted with ease. 'Just keep still, Maggie,' he advised. 'You can't go anywhere with a splinter in your foot and I don't know if you make a habit of slapping men—'

'I don't!' she protested fiercely

'That explains it, then. You failed to realize it's just asking for some comeuppance.' He released her waist and put one arm around her shoulders.

'Come whatance…?' she said with a lot less certainty.

His lips twisted into a wry smile as he looked down into her eyes. 'This, Miss Trent—much pleasanter actually.' He bent his head and teased her lips apart.

It had occurred to Maggie that he was going to kiss her. What hadn't occurred to her was that through her rage and disappointment she could feel any spark of physical attraction, so her confusion was boundless on discovering herself pitched forward into a hot-house of sensual awareness; a sudden, wide open appreciation of Jack McKinnon, the feel of him, the taste of him, the sheer pleasure of him.

This can't be happening to me, she thought, but she was unable to resist the lovely sensations he was arousing in her as he kissed her lips, then her neck and throat, and it was all so warm and close and—most curiously—entirely appropriate.

So appropriate, she didn't protest when he slipped his hand beneath her top and cupped her breasts in their flimsy layer of silk and lace.

She even voiced her approval. 'Mmm…mmm.'

'Nice?' he murmured.

'Very.'

'How about this?' He circled her waist with his arm and started to kiss her deeply.

She clung to him and moved against him, loving the hard strength of his body against hers and becoming extremely aroused, so much so, she doubted her ability to withstand any kind of closure between them other than the final one between a man and a woman.

He was the one who brought them back to earth, slowly, until she was lying in his arms, her eyes dark, her mouth red, her hair gorgeously mussed and her breathing highly erratic.

She blinked several times, her eyes were very green and quite bewildered. 'Where did that come from?'

He smiled and kissed the tip of her nose. 'Powerful emotion often has its other side.'

'You mean being so angry with you made me—I don't know—vulnerable to that?'

'Perhaps.'

'How about you?'

'I—' he paused '—have wanted to do it before. Why don't you finish what you were saying?'

She shook her head. 'I've lost the thread—'

'No, you haven't,' he contradicted. 'You were all set to be extremely passionate about the ''singular difference'' between the facts and what I was implying.'

He was so close she could see the fine laugh lines beside his mouth, a little nick in one of his eyebrows, she could smell soap on his skin and there was a patch of stubble on his jaw his razor had missed.

It came to her with a punch that she'd never looked so closely at a man before, never been interested enough to wonder, for example, how he'd cut his eyebrow and what it would be like to wake up in his arms…

'I…' She tried to collect her thoughts. '*You* seemed to be completely confident I'm one of those predatory girls who won't rest until she gets her man, *plus*—' she looked at him challengingly '—the hoary old spoilt-little-rich-bitch-who-has-to-get-her-own-way bit. That couldn't be further from the way it really is.'

'Which is?' He arched the split eyebrow at her.

'It's never happened to me before,' she said slowly. 'I've always had to fend men off. I've never before been…really, *really* interested. Oh, there've been a few flirtations and I've had some nice friends—Tim is one of them—but you could truthfully say I'm a bit of a novice who's been quite happy…' she sighed and shrugged '…doing my own thing, I guess.'

'Go on.'

'For some…' she paused '…mysterious reason that changed overnight when I was locked in the shed with you. Suddenly I was interested and no one,' she said with emphasis, 'seems to be able to give me one good reason why I shouldn't be, not even *you*, although you dropped me like a hot potato.'

'Maggie—'

'Look.' She laid her hand on his arm. 'Perhaps you are right about me. Perhaps I don't take no for an answer easily, but it's pretty important for me at least to be able to assess what this change means to me.'

He put his finger under her chin and tipped her face up to his.

'In other words…' she smiled fleetingly '…give me one good reason to say to myself, Maggie Trent, you came of age over the wrong man because there's absolutely nothing you can offer him—or there's someone else in his life—and I will go away.'

He stared into her eyes, fingered her chin lightly, then laid his head back with a sigh. 'Your father and I will never see eye to eye—'

'Forget about my father. It so happens I have the same problem with him. And I have taken quite some pains, believe me, to live my life the way I want to rather than the way he wants me to. Yes,' she added intensely, 'it may still be a pretty privileged life compared—perhaps—to how you grew up, if *that's* what you hold against me!'

He smiled slightly. 'No. There's not a lot I have against you, personally.'

'And there's no one else?' she asked seriously.

He watched her for a long moment, then shook his head.

'Well, then.' She gestured. 'Would it be such a bad idea if we got to know each other better?'

'Taking into consideration the fact that I have wanted to kiss you and you don't seem to mind being kissed by me?' he queried.

A glint of laughter shone in her eyes. 'I wasn't going to say that, although I suppose it is fairly pertinent, but there's a lot more to getting to know someone, isn't there?'

If I had any sense, Jack McKinnon mused as he studied the lovely crumpled length of her across his lap, I would end this now, for once and for all.

On the other hand, I did walk away from her and she was the one who wouldn't accept it. Does that absolve me? Not in her father's eyes, I have no doubt. Whichever way I travel with her, to the altar or simply an affair, David Trent is going to hate like hell me knowing his daughter in a biblical sense. But will it be revenge? Only if she falls in love and I don't…

What if I'm right and there's a genuine naivety—and all she's said so far bears that out—that would make it child's play to have her fall in love with me and want to marry me? Talk of revenge or poetic justice, if you like, and there's no doubt the bastard deserves it, but…

'Maggie…' he paused '…what if it doesn't lead towards wedding bells or a relationship, at least?'

She shrugged. 'I don't know—how can I? But the really important thing to me is to know that I didn't sit back and let something I judged special to me just pass me by.'

He grinned suddenly and bent his head to kiss her lightly. 'You're…I don't know, pretty special yourself, I guess.'

'So we could be friends, at least?'

'We could be friends, at least,' he agreed wryly. 'There is a proviso, however.'

'You're not the marrying kind?' she hazarded. She said it perfectly seriously, but there was a glint he was coming to know in her eyes.

'I—'

'I don't know if I am yet,' she interposed. 'Because—and not that this has anything to do with being rich, spoilt and privileged; I'm quite sure I would have been the same if I'd been born in a poorhouse—I can be very dictatorial, I'm told.'

'I wonder why I find that quite easy to believe?' he murmured.

'Some of my actions to date may have led you to suspect it?' she suggested with deep, suspicious gravity.

'One or two.' He circled the outline of her mouth with his finger. 'So how long did you plan to spend up here at the Cape?'

'I booked in for a week, but I have another week's leave up my sleeve. It seemed like a great place, especially for someone dodging journalists and P.I.s, even if you weren't here.'

He narrowed his eyes. 'How *did* you find out about this place?'

'I can't tell you that.' She hesitated. 'But don't worry, it won't go any further.'

He frowned.

'How long are you here for?' she queried.

'Same. Another week,' he said abstractedly.

'When did you arrive?'

'A couple of days ago.'

'Oh, good!' She sat up. 'That gives us plenty of time.'

He removed his arms and folded them across his chest. 'Are you planning to move in with me?'

She thought for a moment, then glinted him an impish glance. 'No. That *would* look as if all I was after was your body.'

'Perish the thought,' he murmured and drew her back into his arms.

'If you're going to kiss me again…' she began.

'I am. You have a problem there?'

'Not *per se*—'

'I'm glad to hear it,' he commented, and ran his fingers down her thigh.

'There is only the fact that—' She stopped and shivered as he stroked her neck and the soft skin just below the neck of her top. 'Uh—the fact that…'

'Go on,' he invited.

'Things could get out of hand rather easily.' She grimaced. 'For me, at least.'

'Then you'll have to rely on me to exert the will-power.'

She eyed him suspiciously. 'Are you laughing at me, Jack?'

'No. Yes,' he corrected himself.

'Am I so—laughable?'

He did kiss her, lightly, his grey eyes gleaming with amusement. 'No. You're unique, that's all.'

She lay back in his arms. 'That's one of the things I like about you.'

He raised an eyebrow.

'I feel safe with you,' she said.

He paused and lifted his head to stare into the distance.

Maggie waited but he didn't enlighten her about whatever he was seeing in his mind's eye. Then, with a strange little sound in his throat, he gathered her very close and kissed her deeply.

Once again it was a sublime experience for Maggie. She felt comforted and cradled but very alive at the same time, and supremely conscious of him, and she uttered a blissful sigh at the end of it that made him laugh.

'The next bit might not be quite as pleasant,' he said, still grinning.

'The next bit?'

'Mmm…' He moved her off his lap and sat her in the corner of the settee. 'Getting rid of the sliver of china in your foot.'

'Oh, that.' She waved a hand. 'I'd forgotten all about it.'

But although he was quick and decisive with his tweezers, she had to sniff back a tear or two as the sliver came out.

'I should have done that the other way around,' he said with a keen glance at her as he bathed her foot in a disinfectant solution.

She raised her eyebrows questioningly.

'Taken it out first and kissed you afterwards,' he elucidated as he peeled open a plaster.

She leant forward and cupped his cheek. 'Kiss me now, quick—and I'll be fine.'

But as his lips rested on hers briefly and they were cool and he smelt of disinfectant she had to resist an almost overwhelming urge to ask for more…

CHAPTER FOUR

THEY had five wonderful days.

They went sailing on his boat, *The Shiralee*, and fishing.

Maggie was in her element on a boat. One thing she did share with her father was a love of the sea and as she was growing up she'd crewed for him.

'I see you know what you're doing,' Jack said to her on their first sail.

'Aye, aye, skipper!' she responded as she turned the boat smartly into the wind so he could set the sails.

He climbed back into the cockpit and put his hands on her waist from behind as she stood at the wheel, and the jib ballooned out in the breeze. 'OK, cut the motor.'

The silence after the motor died was lovely, to be replaced by the equally lovely whoosh of wind in the sails and the rush of water against the hull.

Maggie leant back against him as they braced themselves against the tilt as *The Shiralee* heeled and sped along. 'She sails well,' she said.

He slid his arms around her. 'So she should, I designed her myself.'

Maggie smiled. 'No false modesty about you, Mr McKinnon.'

He turned her around in his arms. 'Not, at least, about boats. You're looking very trim, Miss Trent.'

Maggie glanced down at her short navy shorts and

blinding white T-shirt. She also wore a peaked navy cap with her hair pulled through at the back, and sunglasses. 'A suitably nautical presence for your boat, I hope?' she queried gravely.

'I would say so.' He removed her sunglasses.

Maggie raised her eyebrows.

'Your eyes are amazing. And it is a pleasure to see them not blazing or looking absolute daggers at me,' he said.

A gurgle of laughter rose in her throat. 'That feels like another lifetime ago.'

'On the contrary, it's only a day ago that you slapped my face.'

She coloured and he watched the tide of pink stain the smooth skin of her cheeks. All the same, she said, with an attempt at insouciance, 'Ah—just heat of the moment, I guess.'

'Isn't it always?' he murmured.

Maggie stilled. 'What are you trying to say, Jack?'

His gaze lingered on her face, then he grimaced. 'I'm not sure—'

'That I might be highly impulsive, if not to say irrationally so?'

'As a matter of fact—' he paused '—there is only one "highly" I'm conscious of at the moment in association with you and that's—kissable. How say you, Maggie?'

The growing frown in her eyes was replaced by something quite different. 'Actually, I love the sound of that!'

He laughed and started to kiss her thoroughly until the wind changed and the sails started to flap and they had to draw apart and concentrate on their sailing.

'Goodness, we did come close to those rocks!' Maggie called.

He was reeling in the jib. 'I suspected there was a touch of Delilah in you, now I'm wondering about a siren,' he called back.

Maggie watched him. He was precise and economical in his movements and his physique was breathtaking in khaki shorts and nothing else as he reached up to free a rope.

I knew it, she thought with a sense of satisfaction. There's definitely an action man in there.

There was also, she discovered, an inspired cook within the man.

He'd produced a divine chicken stir-fry served with saffron rice on their first evening together. He grilled fish to perfection. He had a marinade for steak that was to die for. A lot of the food he produced was seafood he'd caught himself—fish, crabs, oysters and painted lobsters.

They explored Bona Bay on Gloucester Island and Breakfast Bay. Once they sailed east through the passage and south to Double and Woodwark Bays and they fished off Edwin Rocks. Maggie caught a Spanish mackerel that day to her intense excitement.

'I've hooked a very large fish, Jack,' she told him as the trolling line she was manning sang out.

'You've probably hooked a rock,' he said prosaically.

'Don't be silly!' She was highly indignant. 'That's no rock! Will you please slow this boat down so I can reel him in?'

Fortunately they were motoring, not sailing, so he was able to stop and drop the anchor and Maggie was able to get the rod out of its holder and start winding in.

'Here, you better let me do it.' He came over to take the rod from her. 'I think it is a fish.'

'I told you so, but it's my fish. Stand aside!'

'Maggie—' he was laughing at her '—you'll never handle it.'

'Oh, yes, I will!'

She nearly didn't. She wound until her arms and shoulders were screaming in pain, and her face grew scarlet.

'Don't bust a gut,' he warned.

'It's nearly in,' she panted. 'Oh, there it is—glory be!' she enthused as the fish leapt out of the water. 'What a beauty!'

'Steady on, now.' He leant over the side of the boat with the gaff in his hands. 'OK! I've got it. Well done!'

Maggie collapsed in a heap and burst into tears.

Jack looked heavenwards, then secured the fish and bent down to scoop her into his arms. He sat down on the padded cockpit seat with her, holding her close. 'You're the most stubborn girl I know,' he said ruefully, 'but I do admire you. Don't cry.' He smoothed the tangle of her hair out of her eyes. 'You won!'

'I know.' She licked some tears from her upper lip and wiped her nose on the back of her hand. 'I just felt very sorry for it all of a sudden. It put up a great fight. I would have liked to let it go.'

'Too late now, but it won't be wasted. Is there any difference between buying fish to eat in a fish shop and catching it yourself?'

She considered. 'No. No, you're right. So you'll cook it?'

'I won't waste a scrap of it,' he promised. 'Even the carcass will be used for the crab pots and I'll reserve some for bouillabaisse.'

'You're a real hunter-gatherer—aren't you?'

'In certain circumstances,' he agreed.

'Good. I like that. Ouch.' She looked at her winding hand. 'This could be a bit sore for a couple of days.'

'I have two temporary solutions.' He picked up her hand and kissed the back of it, then her palm, and gave it back to her. 'The second solution is probably even more efficacious in the short term.'

'Oh, I don't know,' she began. But he sat her on the cushions and disappeared down below. Two minutes later he emerged with a bottle of champagne and two glasses.

He popped the cork ceremonially and poured the champagne. He handed her her glass and raised his to propose a toast. 'To a magnificent fighter!' he said, in the direction of the fish.

'Hear, hear!' Maggie agreed and dissolved, this time, into laughter.

He sat down and put his arm around her shoulders. 'I should have said—to two magnificent fighters.'

She laid her head on his shoulder, feeling more content than she could ever remember.

True to her word, she didn't move in with him, but apart from the hours she slept in her cabin at the resort, often restless hours, the rest of her time was all spent with him.

When they weren't walking, sailing, swimming or

fishing they puttered around his house, they read, they listened to music, they watched DVDs. Her current choice of reading material amused him.

'Don't laugh—I like Harry Potter! And the kids next door are fanatical fans so I have to keep up with the books and we always watch the movies together!'

'Did I say anything?'

'You looked—' She paused. She was snuggled into a corner of one of his settees wearing a long cotton shift, a charcoal background patterned with creamy frangipani flowers. 'You looked *askance*. But I read all sorts of books—crime, romance, adventure, although not science fiction generally.'

'Good.' He returned her gaze with a perfectly straight face.

'Is your taste in literature particularly highbrow?' she queried.

He held up his book cover.

'*Master and Commander*,' she read. 'Surprise, surprise!'

He grinned. 'I like sea stories.'

'That's an understatement. I'd say you have a passion for all things maritime!'

'I do have a couple of other passions,' he objected, and eyed the twisted grace of the way she was sitting with her feet tucked under her.

'Women in general or me in particular?' she asked gravely.

'That's a leading question.' His grey eyes glinted. 'Put it this way, I am enjoying getting to know you better.'

'Same here,' she said. 'I just have this *feeling* that women may come second in your life.'

He shrugged. 'A lot of my design work takes women very much into account,' he said.

'How so?'

'I'll show you.'

First of all he showed her the designs of his catamarans, then he showed her some of his house designs, and she was struck by certain similarities.

'There's absolutely no wasted space,' she said slowly as she studied the floorplan of two admittedly small, compact homes that even had nautical names, The Islander and Greenwich. 'It's all rather shipshape.'

He looked rueful. 'My main ambition was always to design boats.'

'But some of these space-saving ideas are really good. That, plus the fact that they are not shonky…' she paused, then glinted him a wicked little smile '…do take your houses out of the realm of little boxes.'

His lips twitched. 'Thanks, but they still don't fall into the category of your house.'

'For my sins I inherited my house from my grandmother. Where do you live when you're at home?'

'In an apartment at Runaway Bay.'

'A penthouse?' she suggested.

'No.' He grimaced. 'A sub-penthouse.'

'Could we be as bad as each other in the matter of our living arrangements, Mr McKinnon?' she said impishly. 'Incidentally, I don't have a marvellous hideaway on Cape Gloucester.'

'On the other hand, you're likely to inherit a cattle station and more very desirable Gold Coast property, amongst other things.'

Maggie blinked. 'How do you know all that?'

He paused. 'It's fairly common knowledge.'

'I suppose so.' But she frowned, then shrugged. 'I get the very strong feeling my father would dearly love to have a son to bequeath it all to rather than me. He's petrified I'm going to be taken for a ride by a man on the make or I'm going to fritter it all away somehow.'

Jack McKinnon gazed at her so intently, she said, with a comically alarmed expression, 'What have I done now?'

'Nothing.' He rolled up the house plan. As he did so he dislodged a book from the pile on the coffee-table and a photo fell out of it.

Maggie picked it up. 'Who is this?' she asked as she studied the fair, tall woman on board, by the look of it, *The Shiralee*.

'My sister Sylvia,' he said after what seemed to be an unusually long hesitation.

Maggie's eyes widened. 'Your real—'

'No. We're no relation. We were both adopted by the same family as babies. She's a couple of years older but we grew up together as brother and sister. She still lives with our adoptive mother in Sydney, who has motor-neuron disease now. Our adoptive father died a few years ago.'

'That must be why she looks sad,' Maggie commented. 'Lovely but sad. Has she never married?'

'No.' He picked up the ship in a bottle. 'Ever wondered how this is done?'

Maggie blinked at the rather abrupt change of subject, but she said, 'Yes! Don't tell me you did that?'

'I did. I'll show you.'

Cape Gloucester wasn't entirely reserved for relaxation, Maggie found over those days. He kept in touch

with his office by phone and twice a day he spent
some time on his laptop checking out all sorts of mar-
kets: stock, commodity, futures and the like. At these
times he was oblivious to anything that went on
around him.

He was also rather surprised, when she let fall an
idle remark on the subject, to find that she knew her
way around the stock market.

'I'm not just a pretty face, Mr McKinnon,' she assured him with mock gravity, then went on quite seriously to tell him about the portfolio of shares she
was building on her own.

'So it's not only property you dabble—correct
that—you're interested in?' he said.

She directed a cool little glance at him and told
him exactly how much she'd earned in commission
over the past twelve months. 'I do seem to have a
flair for it,' she said with simple honesty.

'You do.' He frowned. 'You also seem to know
your way around these rather well.' He gestured to
the house and boat blueprints he'd shown her.

She told him about the courses she'd done at university.

'All of which,' he said, and smiled suddenly,
'leaves me with egg on my face, I guess.'

Maggie gazed at him, then she said, 'I told you it
was a good idea to get to know me better.'

He laughed. 'You were right.'

She thought, after this conversation, that there was a
subtle shift in their relationship, as if the playing field
had been levelled a little between them, intellectually.

She caught him watching her thoughtfully sometimes, then he invited her to participate when he checked the stock market and some of their discussions on all sorts of things—life, politics, religion—became quite deep.

'Where did you learn to cook like this?' she asked once, halfway through an absolutely delicious seafood crêpe they were having for lunch.

'I grew up in a household where food was important.'

'Your adoptive family?' she queried.

'Yes.'

'Do you...have you...do you know anything about your own family?' she asked tentatively.

'No.' He helped himself to salad and held the salad servers poised above the bowl for a moment. 'I decided—' he lowered the servers gently '—to take the road they took.'

'Which was?' she queried, feeling a little chilled, but not sure why.

'If I wasn't good enough for them, the same applied in reverse.'

He said it quite casually, but she thought she detected a glint of steel in his eyes.

'But,' she heard herself object even although she had the feeling she was trampling on dangerous ground, 'there could have been any number of reasons...I mean, maybe your mother *had* to give you up, for example. I don't think it was as easy to be a single parent thirty-two years ago as it is now. I don't think it's easy *now*, come to that, but there is a lot more support and social security available.'

He sat back with his food untouched and something about him reminded her of the man she'd first met at a jazz concert on a marina boardwalk, very sure of himself, controlled and contained and—as he'd proved then—lethal.

'What would you know about it, Maggie?'

'I—well, nothing, I guess. Look, I'm sorry.' She took a sip of her wine in a bid to hide her discomfort, her discomfort on two fronts. The feeling she'd rushed in where angels feared to tread and her concern for him, she realized with a little rush of amazement. 'I shouldn't pry.' She half smiled. 'Or give gratuitous advice. But—'

'Listen—' he ruffled his hair and pulled his plate towards him '—it's all water under the bridge. It was water under the bridge when I was far too young to understand anything other than the presence of a loving family in my life even if they weren't my own. And that's all that counts really.'

The smile he cast her as he cut into his crêpe was completely serene, and she would have believed him if she hadn't seen that steely, scary glint in his eyes.

He was also quite a handyman, she discovered, and that he set himself an improvement project every time he visited Cape Gloucester.

His current project fitted in with one of Maggie's enthusiasms—gardening. His garden was quite wild and in need of taming, he said. There wasn't much more he could do for it since water was a problem. There was only tank water or extremely salty bore water.

But Maggie was more than happy to pitch in and help him prune and clear away the worst of the tangled overgrowth.

He had a book on the local flora and she also took it upon herself to identify as many of the shrubs as she could. To her delight, she found, amongst the native elms and Burdekin plums, some small trees she identified as *Guettarda Speciosa* that produced sweet-smelling night flowers.

'Listen to this,' she said to him one evening. They were relaxing on the veranda after a divine swim in the high-tide waters only a stone's throw away. The sun had set and he'd lit a candle in a glass and poured them each a gin and tonic in long frosted glasses garnished with slices of bush lemon harvested from a tree in his garden.

'"In India *Guettarda Speciosa* is used for perfume,"' she read from the book.

'How so?'

'Amazingly simply! You throw a muslin cloth over the bush at night so it comes into contact with the flowers. The dew dampens the cloth and it absorbs the perfume from the flowers, then it's wrung out of the muslin in the morning and bingo! You've captured the essence of the perfume.'

'Bingo,' he repeated and watched her idly. She wore a pink bikini beneath a gauzy sarong tied between her breasts. Her golden skin was glowing and her green eyes were sparkling with enthusiasm. 'Let's see if I can anticipate your next question—no, I don't have any muslin cloths.'

Maggie dissolved into laughter. 'How did you know?'

'You're that kind of girl. You like to get out and do things and, the more exotic they are, the better you like it. But despite the absence of muslin...' he leant over the veranda railing and plucked a creamy flower just starting to open '...you could wear a *Guettarda*

Speciosa in your hair.' He leant forward and handed her the flower.

Maggie smelt it. 'Lovely,' she pronounced. 'Thank you.' And she threaded the stem into the damp mass of her hair. 'They do also use it for garlands and hair ornaments in India.'

He smiled and sipped his drink.

'You've read this book, haven't you?' she accused. 'I wasn't telling you anything you didn't know!'

'No. But I've never had a girl to do the honours for before. You look very fetching,' he added.

She studied him. He was sprawled out in a canvas director's chair wearing only a pair of colourful board shorts, and his body was brown, sleek and strong. Coupled with how he was watching her, lazily yet in a curiously heavy-lidded way, the impact on her was one she was becoming very familiar with.

It was as if he could light a spark in her that caused her heart to race, her skin to break out in goose-bumps and a sensual flame to flicker within her just by looking at her. It was also a prelude, she knew, to an intimate moment between them.

Trying to fight it was useless, she'd discovered, although she didn't really understand why she would want to. He'd been as good as his word. He'd taken her to the brink several times, then brought her back, as if he knew she wasn't quite ready to cross that Rubicon. So it had been five days of loving every minute of his company and the things they did, five days of growing intimacy between them—and now this, she thought.

The sudden knowledge that the time was right?

She took a sip of her drink and saw that her hand

wasn't quite steady as it hit her. He hadn't moved at all. How, though, to transmit that knowledge to him?

'I know you think I'm impetuous,' she said huskily, 'and maybe I am, but not over this. I also take full responsibility for my actions. There won't ever be any recriminations.'

He stirred, but said nothing as his gaze played over her.

'Only if *you* want it, of course,' she added, and stumbled up suddenly in a fever of embarrassment— what if he had no idea what she was talking about?

'Maggie…' he got up swiftly and caught her in his arms '…*of course* I want it,' he said roughly, 'but—'

'Oh, thank heavens,' she breathed. 'I've never propositioned a man before—do you mind?' she asked anxiously.

A smile chased through his eyes, but it left them.. bleak? she wondered. Why would that be?

'It's just that some things can never be reversed.' He circled her mouth with his thumb as her lips parted.

'I know that,' she said. 'It doesn't seem to make the slightest difference to how I feel. And if you're trying to say you may not be a marrying man, I may do my darndest to change that, knowing me, but that's…in the future, and what will be will be. Just don't turn your back on me now; I couldn't bear it.'

He stared down into her eyes. They were glimmering with unshed tears like drowned emeralds, but her gaze was very direct and very honest. All the same he held back for some moments longer.

Moments where he thought back over the past days and how he'd had to rein in a growing desire for this girl. Days during which he'd questioned his motives time and again. Times when he'd told himself firmly that she was just another girl, rather touchingly innocent at times, yes, then exceedingly determined at others, but all the same, he could take her or leave her…

He had to doubt that now, in the face of her.. what was the word for it? Gallantry? Yes, and honesty. And what his body most ardently desired. The truth of the matter was, he reflected with a streak of self-directed irony, he could no longer keep his hands off Maggie Trent, or any longer deny himself the final satisfaction of taking her.

'Turn my back on you,' he repeated and released her to cup her face in his hands. 'I couldn't bear it either.' He lowered his head and kissed her.

Maggie clung to him and kissed him back in a fever of relief this time. Then he untied the knot of her sarong and it floated away. Her bikini top suffered the same fate shortly afterwards.

'The perfect gymnast's body,' he murmured as he cupped her high, small breasts peaked with velvety little nipples.

'Thank you.' She drew her hands down his chest and trembled because it felt like a rock wall. Then he was kissing her breasts and sliding his hands beneath her bikini briefs to cup her hips and cradle them against him.

Maggie shivered with delight and she stood on her toes and slid her arms around his neck. 'You do the most amazing things to me,' she said against the corner of his mouth.

He lifted her off her feet and she curled her legs around him. 'If we're not careful this could be over in a matter of seconds,' he replied with a wry little smile and walked inside with her, 'on account of what you do to me.' He nuzzled her neck, then lowered her to the bed.

He turned away and opened a drawer of the bedside table.

'If that's what I think it is,' she said softly, 'you don't need to worry. I'm on the pill—to correct a slight gynaecological problem I have but, according to my doctor, I'm protected against—as he put it— all eventualities.'

Jack looked down at her. 'Is that what you were going to the doctor for the day after we got locked in the shed?'

'Mmm… It's not serious, just a bit debilitating sometimes.'

He lay down beside her and said no more or, she thought dreamily, he let his hands and lips do the talking. He held her and caressed her until she became aware that areas of her body she'd never given much thought to before could become seriously erotic zones beneath his hands and mouth. The nape of her neck, the soft, supple flesh of the inside of her arms, the base of her throat and that pathway that led down to her breasts, her thighs…

She became aware that she could make him catch his breath by moulding herself to him and sliding one leg between his. She discovered that his touch on her nipples sent a thrilling, tantalizing message to the very core of her femininity.

She marvelled at his clean, strong lines and the feel of sleek, hard muscles, and she buried her face in his shoulder with a gasp as he parted her thighs and a rush of warmth and rapture claimed her.

'I just hope you're experiencing what I am,' she breathed as she started to move against him in a rhythm that seemed to come naturally to her. 'It's gorgeous.'

He laughed softly, then kissed her hard. 'To put it mildly, I'm about to die. Ready?'

'Yes, please!'

He claimed her and they rode the waves of their mutual desire to a peak of ecstasy.

They came down from the peak slowly. Their bodies were dewed with sweat and Maggie clung to him as if she were drowning and he was her rock.

'That was…that was…' she said hoarsely, but couldn't go on.

'You're right,' he agreed and kissed her eyelids. 'That was something else. No…' he pushed himself up on his elbow '…pain?'

Her lips trembled into a smile. 'Only the opposite, thanks to you.'

He considered. 'Well, maybe the gymnastics had something to do with it. It's very active.'

'No,' she said firmly, 'it was—*always you*, like the song.'

He grinned. 'OK, I won't argue with you. But if you have any plans to get up and go back to the resort tonight, forget 'em.'

'It was the furthest thing from my mind,' she said dreamily and snuggled up to him.

They slept for a while, then got up and showered, and he made a light supper.

They ate it on the veranda and watched the moon. Then he was struck by an idea. 'Muslin,' he said musingly and picked up her sarong still lying on the veranda floor. 'Anything like this?'

Maggie sat up alertly. 'That's voile and silk, but it's very fine, like muslin—it might just do the trick.'

He looked from the sarong in his hands to the *Guettarda Speciosa* just beyond the veranda railing with the perfume of its night flowers wafting over them in a light breeze. 'How do we anchor it?'

'Clothes pegs?' she suggested.

He nodded and disappeared inside to get them and between them they spread the sarong over the top of the tree.

'Morning will tell,' he commented as he applied the last peg.

'The morning after the night before,' she said with a humorous little glint in her eyes.

'There is that too,' he agreed. 'In the meantime—' he put his hands on her shoulders and drew her against him '—how about back to bed?'

'That sounds like a fine idea to me,' she whispered.

He tilted her chin and looked into her eyes. 'You know what's going to happen, though, don't you?'

She licked her lips. 'Another fine idea by me,' she said softly.

'But what you may not realize,' he temporized, 'is that I suddenly feel like a starving person deprived of a feast.'

She slid her hands around his waist and up his back and pressed her breasts against his chest. 'Who's depriving you of anything?'

He groaned and picked her up.

This time their lovemaking was swift and tempestuous, as if he had felt truly starved of her, but Maggie matched him every inch of the way as the barrier of never having done it before lay behind her and she could express her need of him with a new sureness of touch.

The bed was a tangled mess when they came down from the heights this time, but Maggie was laughing as she caught her breath. 'Wow! I see what you mean.'

He buried his head between her breasts. 'Sorry.'

'Don't be.' She ran her fingers through his hair. 'Let's just call it our epiphany.'

He looked up with something in his eyes she couldn't immediately translate. A tinge of surprise coupled with admiration, she realized suddenly, and it gave her a lovely sense of being on equal terms with him that carried her on to sleep serenely in his arms, once they'd reorganized the bed.

But the next morning it all caught up with Maggie in an embarrassing way.

All her life she'd suffered from a digestive system that took exception to too much excitement and too much rich food.

She woke up feeling pale and shaken and distinctly nauseous. Then she was as sick as a dog.

At first Jack was determined to drive her into the nearest doctor at Proserpine, but she explained between painful bouts of nausea and other complications what the problem was. 'On top of everything else I should have gone easy on the wonderful Mornay sauces and marinades,' she gasped.

He was sitting on the side of the bed watching her with concern. 'Are you sure? You may have picked up a gastric bug.'

'I'm quite sure! A bit of rest, just liquids and plain food for a while and I'll be fine.'

She saw some indecision chase through his eyes and she put her hand over his. 'Really. And I have a remedy I always carry but it's in my luggage back at the resort.'

He came to a decision. 'All right. Do you think you can talk on the phone long enough to tell the resort it's OK to release your vehicle and your luggage to me?'

'Yes.'

Several hours later, she was starting to feel better and Jack McKinnon couldn't have been a better nurse to add to all the other things she admired about him.

He'd made her as comfortable as he could with clean sheets on the bed and a clean nightgown from her luggage. He'd darkened the bedroom section. He'd made up an electrolyte drink for her to replace the minerals she might have lost, and some clear, plain chicken soup. He was as quiet as possible so she could sleep.

And by four o'clock in the afternoon Maggie felt quite human again.

He brought her a cup of black tea and sat on the bed while she drank it.

'I'm too excitable,' she said ruefully. 'That's what my mother puts it down to.'

He gazed at her. She was still pale, but her eyes were clear and she'd brushed her hair into two pony-tails tied with green bobbles.

She could have been about sixteen, he thought, a lovely, volatile child. Yet a brave one who'd matched his ardour in anything but a childlike way until she'd made herself sick.

'I may have been at fault,' he began.

'No. Well—' she smiled faintly '—you could be too good a cook.'

He grimaced. 'What about the rest of it?'

'The way we made love?' She breathed deeply. 'I could never regret a moment of that.'

'Neither could I, but—'

'You're wondering if this is going to happen every time you make love to me? It won't,' she assured him. 'These last few weeks have been—' she gestured '—quite turbulent for me. It was probably bound to happen sooner or later, but I'm feeling—' she chewed her lip '—much more tranquil now.'

He shook his head as if trying to sort through it all.

'But—lonely,' she added softly, 'in this vast bed all on my own.'

'Maggie—'

'If you could just put your arms around me, that would be the best thing that's happened to me today.'

He stared at her and she thought he was going to knock back her suggestion, then he changed his mind.

She sighed with sheer pleasure as he lay down beside her and gathered her close.

'How did the perfume go?' she asked drowsily.

'Your sarong smells lovely, but there was nothing to wring out of it—not enough dew.'

She chuckled. 'We may have to move to India.'

He stroked her hair.

But although they slept in the same bed that night, and although she drew strength and comfort from his arms and it was a magic experience on its own, that was all that happened until the next day when she could demonstrate she was as fit as a fiddle again.

The day after that, on what should have been their last day at Cape Gloucester but they'd made a mutual decision to stay on for a few days more, it all fell apart.

She had no intimation of the drama about to unfold when they swam very early that morning, naked and joyfully.

'This adds another dimension,' she told him as he lifted her aloft out of the sea. She put her hands on his shoulders with her arms straight and her hair dripped over his head. Her skin was covered with goose-bumps and her nipples peaked in the chill of it all.

'Know what?' He tasted each nipple in turn. 'If we hadn't just made love, guess what we'd be doing as soon as we got back? You taste salty,' he added.

She flipped backwards over his encircling arms and wound her legs around him. 'No idea at all!' she said as she floated on her back and her hair spread out on the water like seaweed. 'This water is so buoyant.'

'And you're particularly buoyant this morning, Miss Trent,' he teased. 'Not to mention full of cheek.'

She arched her body, then flipped upright, laughing down at him. 'I wonder why?' She sobered and stroked his broad shoulders. 'What is the masculine equivalent of a siren?'

'There isn't one.'

'There should be,' she told him. 'Anyway, you're it, Mr McKinnon. Enough to make any girl feel very buoyant, not to mention—wonderful!'

He stared into her eyes, as green as the sea at that

moment, with her eyelashes clumped together and beaded with moisture, and at the freshness of her skin. And he said with an odd little smile, as if there was something in the air she wasn't aware of, 'I haven't felt quite so wonderful myself for a while.'

She insisted on cooking breakfast, saying it was about time she earned her keep.

They'd showered together and she'd put on a short denim skirt with a green blouse that matched her eyes. Her hair was loose as it dried and she frequently looped it behind her ears as she cooked—grilled bacon and banana with chopped, fried tomato and onion and French toast.

'There,' she said proudly as she set it out on the veranda table. 'I may not be in your gourmet class, but I'm not useless in the kitchen either.'

'Did I say you were?' he drawled.

She pulled out a chair and wrinkled her nose at him. 'You've carefully avoided any mention of it, which led me to wonder if you'd simply assumed my privileged background had left me fit only to rely on someone else to provide my meals—what a mouthful, Maggie,' she accused herself with a gurgle of laughter.

He grinned. 'I did wonder.'

'Well, now you know. I'm actually quite domesticated.' She picked up her knife and fork, then paused and frowned. 'Was that a car in the driveway I heard?'

He cocked his head. 'I'm not expecting anyone.'

A moment later they heard a door bang, then footsteps crunching on the gravel path around the side of the house.

'Anyone home?' a voice called at the same time as a tall fair woman appeared at the bottom of the steps, then, 'Oh, Jack! I'm so glad I caught you. Maisie did say you'd decided to stay on for a couple more days, but one never quite knows with you!'

To Maggie's surprise, Jack McKinnon went quite still for a long moment, still and tense and as dangerously alert as a big jungle cat. Then he relaxed deliberately and stood up. 'Sylvia,' he said. 'This is a surprise.'

Maggie blinked and Sylvia, his adoptive sister, arrived on the veranda. She was as lovely as her photo and there was no trace of sadness about her as she greeted Jack, full of laughing explanations.

'I really needed a bit of time off—Mum and I were getting to the stage of wanting to shoot each other! So I flew up to Proserpine yesterday, hired a car and took off before dawn hoping to catch you and surprise you—oh!' Her gaze fell on Maggie. 'Oh, I'm so sorry. Maisie didn't say anything about…' She trailed off awkwardly.

'Don't be silly, Syl,' Jack said quietly. 'I'm always happy to see you. This is Maggie.'

Maggie got up and came round the table, holding out her hand. 'Maggie Trent, actually. How do you do?'

Sylvia's mouth fell open, as if she was completely floored, and she appeared not to notice Maggie's proffered hand. Instead, her gaze was riveted on Maggie's tawny hair and green eyes. Then she closed her mouth with a click. 'Not—Margaret Leila Trent?'

'Why, yes!' Maggie beamed at her. 'I don't know how you know that, but that's me.'

'Jack,' Sylvia said hollowly, and turned to him,

'don't tell me this is what I think it is. He'd…' she swallowed visibly '…he'd kill you if he knew…'

'Who?' Maggie said into the sudden deathly silence.

'Your father,' Sylvia whispered. Then she put a hand to her mouth and turned around to run down the steps.

'You stay here, Maggie,' Jack ordered. 'I'll be back as soon as I can.' He followed Sylvia.

CHAPTER FIVE

IT WAS an hour before he came back, a tense, highly uncomfortable hour for Maggie.

She got rid of their uneaten breakfasts and tidied up, but there was a dreadful feeling of apprehension at the pit of her stomach and all her movements were jerky and unco-ordinated.

As far as she was aware he'd never met her father, so what could be involved? Then her mind fastened on something he'd said the day she'd found him here. Something about men and their grievances not being parted lightly.

She'd assumed when he'd said that, and something else she remembered about never seeing eye to eye with her father, that her father's arrogant, high-handed reputation and the ruthless businessman he could be, also by repute, were the things Jack McKinnon took exception to…

Then she remembered his reluctance—she put her hands to her suddenly hot cheeks—to have anything more to do with her after the shed incident. What had she precipitated?

When he came back she was sipping coffee, but sheer nerves made her rush into speech. 'What's going on? How is she? Where is she?'

There was a plunger pot on the veranda table and another mug. He poured coffee for himself in a completely unsmiling way that terrified Maggie all the more.

'She's booked into the resort for the time being. Maggie, believe me…' he pulled out a chair and sank into it '…I would rather—climb Mount Everest—than be the one to tell you this, but since you're here, and this has happened, I don't seem to have any choice.'

'No, you *don't*,' she agreed. 'You obviously *know* my father!'

'Not well,' he said rather grimly. 'Sylvia is the one who knows him, or knew him. They had an affair—' He stopped abruptly at the shocked little sound she made.

'It's common enough,' he said then.

'Well, yes.' She paused and laced her fingers together. 'And my parents haven't—it doesn't exactly seem to be a joyful marriage at times, but they are together so—' She broke off and looked at him with a painful query in her eyes.

'Your father desperately wanted a son and your mother couldn't have any more children.'

A bell rang in the recesses of Maggie's mind. Something her grandmother had said to her, then never explained. Something in response to *her* saying she should have been a boy. *Don't go down that road, Maggie. Your mother has and…* But Leila Trent had never completed the statement.

She blinked several times as she looked back down the years, and it all fell into place. The growing tension between her parents, her mother's anguish, carefully concealed so that her growing daughter would not be affected, but now it came back to Maggie in a hundred little ways… How could she have been so blind? she wondered.

She cleared her throat. 'Go on.'

'Your father met Sylvia about six years ago. They fell in love—at least Sylvia assures me they did. She…' he paused and looked out over the glittering sea with his eyes hard and his mouth set '…fell for him in a big way despite his being married.'

'Did…did he offer to leave my mother and marry her?'

'He certainly led her to expect it. Then things changed dramatically.' He turned back to her. 'Talking of gynaecological problems, Sylvia has had more than her fair share of them and the net result is that she's unable to have children. When your father discovered that, the terms of his proposition changed somewhat. There was no more talk of marriage.'

Maggie went pale.

'I guess,' he said slowly, 'I need to fill you in on a bit of background here. Possibly because we were both adopted—there was never any secret made of it—we had more common ground than many siblings have, Sylvia and I. We looked out for each other as we were growing up. There were times when we almost seemed to be on the same wavelength like twins. So I knew exactly how Sylvia was going through the mill with your father. And I knew she was too loving, too special to be any man's mistress.'

'Did she agree with you?' Maggie asked.

He shrugged. 'Pertinent question. Did I rush in and sort out her life as *I saw fit*?'

'Did you?'

'No. To give your father his due, he was infatuated. Sylvia took the first steps to break it off herself, but he wouldn't hear of it. She finally came to me and begged for help. She said she doubted she would ever love anyone quite like that again, but the sense of inadequacy she felt—your mother may have had the same problem—over this inability to provide sons was crippling her and she had to get out.'

'You…you confronted him?' Maggie hazarded.

He smiled unamusedly. 'Yes.'

'How did you make him see sense?'

Jack stared at her. 'I threatened him with exposure to his wife and his, at the time, seventeen-year-old daughter. You may not realize this, Margaret Leila Trent, but your father, for all his sins and his thirst for a son, loves you dearly. He often talked to Sylvia about you with a great deal of pride.'

There were tears running down Maggie's cheeks. 'I didn't know,' she whispered. She stood up and walked to the veranda railing. 'It's all so sad!' She dashed her cheeks. 'My mother *still* loves him, I'm sure. Sylvia…?' She turned back with a question in her eyes.

'Sylvia went to hell and back.'

Maggie sniffed. 'And that's all you had to do to get him to stop seeing her?'

He folded his arms. 'Yes, but it didn't end there. We've been playing a game of tit for tat ever since.'

Her eyes widened. 'How so?'

'He tried to ruin me financially.' This time his smile was pure tiger. 'But two can play that game, as he's found to his cost several times.'

Maggie sank back into her chair and dropped her face into her hands. 'That's horrible.' She swallowed, then looked up. 'Of course. That explains the revenge element.'

He didn't deny it. He was silent for so long, Maggie found it difficult to breathe as she wondered what was coming.

'It crossed my mind,' he said and grimaced. 'More than once. That is why, Maggie,' he said slowly, 'I dropped you like a hot potato, or tried to.'

She bit her lip and coloured. 'You could have told me this a lot sooner.'

'It was hard enough to tell you now.' He gestured. 'But in the end revenge didn't come into it.' His lips twisted. 'You may be a right chip off the old block in some respects, but in others you're very sweet and lovely and refreshing and I...' he paused '...I just couldn't resist you even although I knew damn well I should.'

'I didn't give you much choice,' she said bravely. 'I...was just like the women who ride off into the sunset with you because they can't help themselves.'

He looked comically confused. 'What women?'

She waved a hand. 'Doesn't matter—'

'I've never ridden off into the sunset with a woman against her better judgement,' he protested. 'I've never "ridden" off with anyone.'

A spark of irritation lit Maggie's eyes. 'Will you leave it? It's just something I thought to myself once, in relation to you, that's all.'

A trickle of understanding came to his eyes. 'I see. Sorry, that was a bit dense.'

'Yes, it was. So, what are we going to do now?'

He finished his coffee and sat back, then, 'You may like to think the responsibility is yours, but it isn't, it's mine, and only I can redeem things. Go back to your family, Maggie, and forget me, otherwise you'll be torn to pieces,' he said very quietly.

'I...my father...' She couldn't go on and her throat worked.

'In a sense I'm as bad as he is,' he pointed out.

'He's also a man to whom sons may legitimately mean a lot, it is quite an empire and a very old name. Mid-life crises can happen to the best of married men and Sylvia is gorgeous. He—'

'Don't,' Maggie begged. 'Don't make any more excuses for him for *my* sake and if you don't mean them. Do you really think any better of him?'

He watched her impassively, then shook his head.

'The other thing is, only—' she pointed to sea where they'd swum '—a couple of hours ago we…we were…' Once again tears started to roll down her cheeks.

'You may never know how hard this is, Maggie,' he said abruptly, 'but one day you'll be grateful. Can you imagine having to tell your mother why your father hates me the way he does?'

That stopped Maggie in her tracks. 'Maybe she knew but decided to live with it?' she whispered.

He shook his head. 'From his reaction when I delivered my threat I could see that neither of you knew.'

Maggie made one last effort. 'What if Sylvia hadn't turned up or found out about me for, well, ages?'

He ran his hand through his hair and sighed. 'No doubt I'd have come to my senses before that.'

'Has this—has ''us'' meant anything to you at all, Jack?'

Her hands were lying helplessly on the table and he reached over to cover one of them with his own. 'Yes, it has, but I'm not the right man for you.'

'Why not? Apart from everything else.'

'You can't separate them, Maggie.' He hesitated, then shrugged. 'I just don't think I'd take well to domesticity.'

'A loner?'

He narrowed his eyes and looked past her. 'That's how I started out in this life. But—' he withdrew his gaze from the past and concentrated on her again '—for the *right* man,' he stressed, 'you're going to be a wonderful wife. A bit of a handful, prone to some excesses like locking people in sheds and—'

She pulled her hand away and stood up as his words acted like a catalyst. She wiped her face with her fingers, but although the tears subsided her heart felt as if it were breaking and all the fight drained out of her.

If he could even *think* of her with another man after what had passed between them, she had to believe that all he felt for her was a passing attraction.

Yes, maybe there was affection too, but not the conviction she held. The conviction that she'd fallen deeply in love with him. Not the pain at the prospect of being parted from him, nor the sheer agony of thinking of him with another woman...

No, she had to believe it hadn't happened for him as it had happened for her and—talk about being torn between him and her family—that would really tear her apart, going on with him under those circumstances.

And she remembered her original proposition—she would take full responsibility for her actions and there would be no recriminations. But how to act on those brave words? something within her cried.

She drew a trembling breath. 'What do they say? You live and learn.' She smiled, but she couldn't eradicate the bitterness from it. 'I'll go now,' she added simply.

He stood up and watched her like a hawk for a moment. 'Will you be all right?'

She cast him a look tinged with irony.

'Look, I know—'

'This will take a bit of getting over?' she suggested. 'Of course.' And she squared her shoulders and tilted her chin at him with further, this time patent irony. 'But I am a Trent, after all.'

'Maggie,' he said exasperatedly, 'I meant will you be all right physically? I long since stopped classing you with your father.'

'Perhaps you shouldn't have, Jack. Physically? Oh, you mean…? Well, I should be fine on both those fronts. I am on the pill and I've been careful about what I ate after the other day. No, I'll be fine.'

She stopped and stared at him. 'Provided I do this very quickly,' she said barely audibly and stood on her toes to kiss him briefly. 'You were…you were everything a girl could pray for. Take care.' She turned away and went inside. He moved, then stilled.

It took her all of five minutes to stuff her possessions into her bag and he carried it to her car.

She said goodbye unemotionally and he did the same. She even drove off with a wave. Two miles down the road she pulled up and was overcome by a storm of weeping and disbelief—how could it have ended like this?

To coin a phrase, she returned to the bosom of her family for a few days despite the new ambivalence of her feelings for her father, but some things had changed, she discovered.

Something in her mother's voice, when she rang her to say she was home, alerted her to it. A new lightness, a younger-sounding voice—I must be imagining it, Maggie thought—but when Belle suggested a family reunion on the cattle station, Maggie gave it some thought. The fact that her father was home had her in two minds, though.

Would she find herself unable to hide her hatred for his actions and the misery they'd caused her and Sylvia McKinnon? Was there any way she could heal the breach between David Trent and Jack McKinnon so there need not be this misery, for her, anyway? Come to that, could she hide her misery and despair from her mother?

In the end her curiosity got the better of her and she used the last few days of her leave to drive up to Kingaroy and the sprawling old wooden homestead, over a hundred years old but now extensively modernized, that had been the birthplace of the Trent dynasty.

She needn't have worried about hiding anything from her parents. By some miracle the breach had been healed. They were in love again and, despite observing the usual courtesies, there might have been only the two of them on the planet.

I don't believe this, Maggie thought. What has happened?

She watched them carefully, especially her father. The tawny hair was a little grey, he was close to fifty now, but even so he was attractive—it was not hard to see how he would have appealed to Sylvia six years ago despite a twenty-year age gap. And as always, when he set himself to be pleasant, he was more than that. He was vital, funny—entirely engaging, in fact, until you ran into the brick wall of the other side of his personality, the high-handed, arrogant side she had clashed with frequently down the years.

To her confusion, however, the weight of Jack's revelations didn't add a black hatred to her difficult feelings for her father.

Because she was so happy to see him making her mother happy again? she wondered.

Because a certain streak of common sense told her there were always two sides to a story such as— Sylvia had known her father was a married man and should have thought twice about breaking up any-one's marriage?

Because David Trent had conveyed enough admi-ration of her, his daughter, to someone else even al-though his thirst for a son had driven him to betraying her mother?

I don't know what to think, she acknowledged. I'm all at sea. What would happen if I told him about Jack and tried to smooth things between them? In this new mood he's in, maybe I could?

But something held her back. Would Jack McKinnon want her permanently in his life under any circumstances? She had strenuously to doubt it. As for her feelings for Jack, she just didn't know where she stood there at all.

Her mother did come down from her cloud nine briefly as Maggie was leaving.

'Darling, are you all right?' she asked anxiously as they were walking to the car. Maggie had taken leave of her father earlier. 'You still seem a little quiet.'

'I'm fine.' Maggie gestured to take in the wide blue sky and the vast dusty paddocks, and artfully changed the subject. 'I don't know how this happened.' She

turned to Belle and put her arms around her. 'But I'm
very happy for you, Mum. You're looking so beautiful.'

Belle trembled in her daughter's arms. 'You can
tell?'

'See those steers in the paddock? They could tell,'
Maggie said humorously but lovingly. She disen-
gaged and got into her car. 'Take care of each other,'
she added with a wave, and drove off.

She went back to work.

A month after her stay at Cape Gloucester, she
went to see her doctor with an incredulous question.

'I thought you told me I was covered against all
eventualities?'

'Sit down, Maggie,' he invited. 'What do you
mean?'

'I'm pregnant! It's the only explanation I can think
of, but I never once forgot to take my pills.'

The doctor digested this and said slowly, 'It was a
low-dose pill. Sometimes they're not infallible, as I'm
sure I told you—not that we were discussing them so
much as a contraceptive at the time, but as a means
of helping you with difficult periods. Have you had
any cataclysmic upsets?'

Maggie closed her eyes and thought of explaining
that she'd fallen in love overnight, she'd pursued her
man relentlessly and given him little choice about taking her to bed—events that had gone around and
around in her mind and pointed an accusing finger at
her each and every time.

'Gastric upsets or the like?' the doctor added.

Her lashes flew up.

'I did mention how they could interfere with the pill,' he said gently.

Maggie put a hand to her mouth. 'I forgot all about that. I…I…was so carried away I didn't even think of it,' she admitted. 'Oh, what a fool I've been!'

'Tell me all about it,' he invited.

Half an hour later, still in a state of shock, she drove home.

The doctor's advice had been copious. Termination was her choice, but even the thought of it was horrific. If she didn't go ahead with that, the father of the child she was carrying deserved to know about it and no child should be completely deprived of its father even if circumstances prevented its parents from living together. And in that event, she should seek moral support from her family.

'If only you knew,' she murmured as she unlocked her front door. 'If only you knew! On the other hand, termination is out of the question, so…'

Three weeks later she was still grappling with her problems on her own when fate took a hand.

The property that had started it all was now officially on the market. It had been advertised and there'd been quite a bit of interest—none from the McKinnon organization or anyone bearing that name, however.

Maggie had been happy to be able to distance herself from it. As the agent who'd received the initial enquiries from the owners it should have been her 'baby'. In other words, even if another on their team sold it, she would still be entitled to some of the commission, but she'd waived that right when she'd taken four weeks' unexpected leave.

But there came a day when a woman rang in requesting an inspection and Maggie was the only one available to do it. Very conscious of the strain she'd put on the team with her unexpected leave, she temporized, then knew she should do it.

She arranged to meet the woman on the property at four in the afternoon and made a note of her name—a Ms Mary Kelly.

It wasn't as beautiful a day as the day she'd met Jack McKinnon on this little bit of heaven, Maggie thought as she pulled her car up behind a smart blue BMW. There were dark clouds chasing across the sky and a threat of rain, but it was still lovely.

She got out and went to meet Ms Kelly, a smartly groomed woman in her forties who also sparkled with intelligence and had a decisive air about her.

As they began their inspection Maggie said, 'Do you intend to live here, Mary?' They'd quickly got onto first-name terms.

'No. I'm doing this inspection on behalf of a— friend,' Mary replied. 'A second opinion is always helpful, isn't it?'

Maggie agreed, but realized suddenly that her usual 'selling persona' wasn't quite in place because she wasn't feeling very well. She struggled on, however. She dredged up several ideas she had for the house, she enthused about the creek, she was just about to suggest a tour of the shed when a violent bout of nausea overtook her and she had to run for a clump of trees where she proceeded to lose her lunch and afternoon tea.

Mary was most concerned and helpful. She dipped

her scarf in the creek, wrung it out and offered it to
Maggie to wipe her face and hands.

'Thank you,' Maggie breathed and patted her face
with the cool cloth gratefully.

'Something you ate?' Mary Kelly suggested.

'No.' Maggie shook her head, and for some reason,
maybe because she'd told no one but her doctor, it
all came tumbling out. 'I'm pregnant and this is, so
I'm told, morning sickness in the afternoon.' She grimaced ruefully.

'You poor thing,' Mary said slowly and with a
gathering frown.

'Oh, it hasn't been too bad! It just..catches me unawares at times. There.' She rinsed the scarf thoroughly and handed it back. 'Thanks so much—unless
you'd rather I kept it and sent it back to you properly
laundered? Oh, by the way, no one at the office knows
about it yet so—'

'I won't tell them,' Mary promised. 'Are you sure
you're all right now?'

'Fine! Would you like to see the shed?'

'No, thank you, I think I've seen enough. Uh...'
Mary hesitated as if she had her mind on other mat-
ters, then she said, 'Is there much interest in the property?'

'Quite a lot, I believe, although there've been no
offers yet.'

'Do you think the owners have much up their
sleeve—are prepared to negotiate, in other words?'

'Look, I'm not sure about that. I did have it orig-
inally, but Mike Davies is now the agent in charge,
so to speak, only he wasn't available this afternoon.
What say I get him to give you a call?'

'That would be fine, Maggie. Now you take care! How far along are you?'

'Roughly two months.' Maggie held out her hand. 'Nice to meet you, Mary.'

They parted and Maggie drove home slowly. Although she hadn't got to the shed, the whole exercise had woken all sorts of memories in her and reactivated all sorts of heartaches to fierce and hurtful from the dull pain they'd coagulated into.

She also knew she would have to make some kind of a decision very shortly. Follow her doctor's advice or go into hiding and cope with it all on her own?

In fact, there was only one lessening of the tension for her, and that was her growing curiosity about the baby. And the thought that it might fill the gap in her life Jack McKinnon had created.

She showered and changed into loose long cotton trousers and a long white shirt as the threat of rain earlier became a reality and thrummed on the roof in a series of heavy showers.

She made herself an early dinner, a snack really, of toasted cheese and a salad. She was just sitting down to eat it when her doorbell rang.

Her eyes widened in shock as she opened the door and Jack stood there.

'You!' she breathed and clutched her throat.

'Yes,' he agreed dryly. 'Let me in, Maggie. It's wet out here.'

'Of course.' She stood aside. 'But what are you doing here?'

'Come to see you,' he said briefly. 'Brrr… It's not only wet, there's a distinct tinge of winter in the air.'

'Come into the lounge. It's warm in there.'

He followed her through, then eyed her snack on the coffee-table next to the TV remote.

'I'm not very hungry,' she said defensively.

He looked around the lovely room, then his gaze came back to her and he looked her up and down comprehensively. 'How are you?' he asked abruptly.

She moved and pushed her hands behind her back because they were shaking. Nothing had changed about him, although he was more formally dressed than she'd ever seen him in a beautiful charcoal suit with a pale grey shirt and a bottle-green tie with anchors on it.

But his clothes didn't change him. They added a kind of 'high boardroom flyer' touch, but they didn't disguise the perfection of his physique. His streaky fair hair was shorter and tamed, but he still had a tan, and she could see him in her mind's eyes, aboard *The Shiralee* wearing only shorts…

She couldn't read his grey eyes at all—why had he come? Was it to say—*I made a mistake, Maggie. I can't live without you…?*

'Maggie?'

'I'm fine,' she said jerkily. 'Sit down. Would you like something?'

'No, thanks. Don't let your supper get cold.'

'Oh, that's all right.' She sat down and pushed the plate away.

He sat down opposite and studied her penetratingly. Then he said quietly, 'Any news?'

Foolishly, her mind went quite blank. What's he asking me? she wondered. How can there be any news? He was the one who sent me away… 'No,' she said bewilderedly.

His mouth hardened for some reason. 'I'd more or

less made up my mind to buy that property, you know.'

Maggie blinked. 'The one…?'

'The one with the shed that was hijacked to house a stolen vintage car and bike; the one you locked us into,' he said deliberately.

She blushed.

'But I decided to get a second opinion,' he went on, 'from someone whose judgement I value.'

'A second opinion,' Maggie repeated as the words struck a chord in her mind and it started to race.

'Yes,' he agreed. 'I think Maisie's name has cropped up between us before. She's my right-hand man. I rely on her extensively.'

Maggie blinked furiously. 'But there's no Maisie at the McKinnon Corporation, I checked,' she blurted out, then her cheeks burnt even more fierily. 'I mean—'

'That's because I'm the only one at the office who calls her Maisie. Her real name…' he paused and their gazes clashed '…is Mary Kelly.'

Maggie froze. 'She…she told you?' she breathed.

'Yes.'

'But that's not fair! I had no idea who she was. I would *never* have—' She stopped abruptly.

'Told her you were pregnant otherwise? How about telling me? I gather you hadn't planned to do that either.'

Maggie got up and paced around in deep agitation with the bottom line being—*So much for the I can't live without you, Maggie, bit.*

Then she turned to him incredulously. 'How would she know it was your baby?'

'She didn't. But she did know about what happened

in the shed because I alerted her to be on the lookout for any unforeseen complications while I was away. When she came back to me with her report this afternoon, she told me it was you who'd shown her around—and the rest of it.'

Silence stretched between them until he added, 'I was the one left to put two and two together—although Maisie is very adroit at reading between the lines.'

Maggie sat down again suddenly. 'When I said there was no news, I think I must have been still in shock at seeing you again. My mind just went blank.'

'OK, reasonable enough. What about the two months prior to tonight?'

Maggie rubbed her face, then she laced her fingers and said urgently, 'I just haven't known what to do!'

'How did it happen?' he queried grimly. 'You seemed so certain you were safe; you *told* me you were on the pill.'

'I was,' she said hollowly and explained what must have happened.

'Do your parents know?'

'No.'

He stared at her, taking in the faint shadows beneath her eyes and her slender figure beneath the long white shirt and flimsy trousers. There was no sign of any changes in her as yet—or, yes, there was, he thought suddenly. There was a new air of vulnerability about her.

'There's only one thing to do,' he said. 'The sooner you marry me, the better.'

CHAPTER SIX

MAGGIE reached towards her plate and took a carrot stick out of the salad, a purely reflex action as the impact of what Jack had said hit her.

Then she stared at him with the wand of carrot in one hand and her mouth open.

A glint of humour lit his eyes. 'A curious reaction. I can't read it at all.'

She closed her eyes. 'That's because I can't read my emotions at the moment at all.' Her lashes lifted. 'You're not serious?'

'Oh, yes, I am.'

'But, apart from all the complications you so carefully pointed out to me at Cape Gloucester, you don't particularly want to marry anyone, do you? Unless that was a sop to my sensibilities, but that's even worse because it means you particularly didn't want to marry me!'

'Eat the carrot or put it down, Maggie,' he suggested.

She stared at him, then threw it down on the plate because a moment or so ago she might have been shell-shocked and unable to get in touch with her emotions—that could have been true of her for the last two months, she realized—but she was no longer.

Jack McKinnon had hurt her almost unbearably, she now knew. Yes, a lot of it was her own fault, but that didn't alter her vulnerability to this man, and to let him marry her only because of their baby—was that asking for *more* hurt than she could bear?

'I got myself into this,' she said. 'I will handle it.'

This time it was a glint of anger that lit his eyes. 'Don't go all proud "Trent" on me, Maggie,' he warned. 'If you think that I, of all people, would allow you to wander off into the sunset with a child of mine, think again.'

Her eyes widened as she realized what he was saying, but there was more.

'If you think I would allow a child of mine to be swallowed up in the midst of *your* family—that is also simply not on the cards.'

She swallowed a couple of times. 'Look, I know that as an adoptee yourself you…you must feel pretty strongly about this, but I would never deny you access to your child—'

'And do you think you're strong enough to hold out against your father, Maggie, if he sees things differently? I don't. So we'll both be there for it, whether you like it or not.'

She stood up tensely. 'It's not a question of liking it or not! What I'm talking about is a shotgun marriage—'

'That is another possibility.' He lay back in his chair and steepled his fingers. 'You could find your father does come after me with a shotgun.'

'Nonsense!'

'I'm speaking metaphorically, but marriage, even to me, may be his preferred option for his only daughter rather than single motherhood.'

It came to Maggie in a blinding flash that perhaps even her sanity and therefore the welfare of her baby could be at risk if she allowed herself to become a pawn between these two powerful, arrogant men. Yes, two—I was right about you in the first place, Jack McKinnon! she said to him in her mind.

She put her hand on her flat stomach, thought of the life within her, and breathed deeply. Then she picked up the cordless phone on the coffee-table, and she dialled the Kingaroy homestead number, where she knew her parents were still holidaying.

She suffered a moment of anguish while the phone rang at the thought of their, particularly her mother's, new happiness, but how happy would either of them be if she ran away?

'Dad?' she said when her father answered. 'It's Maggie. Will you please just listen to me? I happened to meet and have an affair with a man you detest, Jack McKinnon. I know what all the bad blood is about, but I will *never* let Mum know. Unfortunately—'

She paused and listened for a while, then, 'Dad, please, if you love me at all, just listen. I was the one who did the chasing, not Jack. Unfortunately, and this was also my own fault entirely, I'm pregnant. Jack has decided I should marry him although our affair was—completely over before I realized I was pregnant. But while I'm immensely concerned about this baby's welfare, I don't think a loveless marriage is the solution—'

Once again she broke off and listened, then, 'No, Dad, I won't be doing that either. I appreciate your concern but this is the point I need to make you both understand—neither of you can make me do anything. In fact, if you continue this feud and—' she raised her eyes to Jack's '—either of you make my life unbearable, I'll go away where neither of you can find me.'

Her eyes didn't leave Jack's face while she listened again, then she looked away and said into the phone, 'I'm *sorry*, Dad, I know this must have come as a shock. Please break it gently to Mum. I love you both, but I meant every word I said.' She put the phone down.

Jack stirred at last. 'Was that slamming the shed door well and truly, Maggie?'

She shrugged. 'I've been living in a terrible vacuum since I found out. How to tell you? How to tell them? What to do? Until it suddenly came to me I'm no one's hostage and what I'll be doing is staying right here and continuing my job as long as I'm able, and letting this baby grow in peace. Yes, I was angry,' she conceded.

'Who's to say it would be a loveless marriage?' he queried.

'Jack—' she rubbed her face wearily '—you have given me absolutely no indication to the contrary—'

'Because I didn't burst in on you and sweep you into my arms?' he asked. 'Your father isn't the only one to get a shock today.'

She rubbed her knuckles on her chin. 'I know. I'm sorry.' She gestured helplessly.

'As a matter of fact, the thought of my own child has had a rather startling effect on me.'

'Me too,' she conceded. 'I mean, it could probably be quite an interesting child.' A ghost of a smile touched her lips.

'It would certainly give us a lot of common ground.'

His words hung in the air, but Maggie was too tired

and emotionally wrung out to continue the contest. She simply stared at him with deeper shadows etched beneath her eyes and her face very pale.

He frowned, then he got up and came round to her. He took her hand and drew her to her feet.

'You're extraordinarily brave and feisty, Maggie, but you don't have to bear this burden on your own. No,' he said as her lips parted, 'don't say anything now. But I do have your welfare, just as much as the baby's, very much at heart. Think that over, but, in the meantime, get a good night's sleep.'

His lips twisted, then he went on, 'It may have been equivalent to slamming the shed door, but you certainly cleared the air.' He kissed her gently. 'I'll see myself out. By the way, don't forget to eat. It's important now.'

Maggie inhaled deeply as he walked away from her, and closed her eyes. The brush of his lips on hers had taken her right back to Cape Gloucester and the times she'd spent in his arms and his bed.

'I really loved you, Jack McKinnon, but I don't believe you will ever really love me because if it hadn't been for—fate—you would never have come back to me,' she whispered. 'That is so sad.'

Despite the deep well of sadness she felt, after taking the phone off the hook, she went to bed and slept like a top, the first time for ages. This was just as well since her mother and father arrived on her doorstep early the next morning.

Over the next days Maggie continued resolutely along the course she'd set for herself.

She told Jack that she still couldn't see her way clear to marrying him because—apart from anything else and there was plenty of that!—if he hadn't seen himself as the right man for her before, a baby wasn't going to change things.

He took it with surprising equanimity, although she intercepted one tiger-like little glance from him that seemed to say, We'll see about that. But she didn't see it again and she decided she'd imagined it.

She told her parents that they had to accept the fact that she'd come of age in her own way and she'd made her own mistakes. She told them that Jack would always be a part of her life now because of their child and would they please, please make the best of it.

It was her mother who surprised her. To her intense relief none of the new closeness between her parents seemed to have been lost beneath the weight of her news. But while her father's face changed and hardened at every mention of Jack's name, Belle, if she felt any animosity towards the man responsible for this contretemps, didn't show it.

Then she took Maggie aside and said to her quietly, 'I know all about it now.'

Maggie stared at her. 'You mean…you mean…?'

'Sylvia McKinnon?' Belle nodded. 'Your father, well, we'd been at odds for some time before it happened. I felt inadequate and angry because I knew how much he longed for a son, he felt guilty and defensive and it coloured our whole relationship. I knew he was restless and unhappy six years ago and that there was probably another woman in his life although I didn't know—I didn't want to know who it was.'

Belle paused and Maggie spoke. 'You're making it

sound as if Dad—as if *you* were the one at fault; that's crazy!'

'Darling…' Belle smiled a little painfully '…I know that, but sometimes these urges are so powerful in men you can't fight them. The important thing is, your father finally fought it himself and he's come back to me. In many ways we're happier now than we've ever been.'

Maggie stared down at her hands a trifle forlornly.

'There is still,' Belle said, 'the problem of Jack McKinnon.'

'I know. Men don't part with their grievances towards each other lightly.'

'You're not wrong!' Belle looked humorous. 'Tell me about him? By the way, I may not get your father to do this yet, but I intend to meet him.'

Maggie hesitated, then she told her mother everything. 'Of course this is only between you, me and the gatepost,' she finished.

'Of course. So you fell in love but he didn't?'

Maggie got up and wandered over to the window. They were in her bedroom on the second floor and she looked down over her colourful garden. 'Yes,' she said at last. 'That's why I can't accept second-best from him.'

A week later her mother did meet Jack and, although it had to be inherently awkward and there was a certain reserve that Maggie detected in Belle, it went well. Jack was quiet but courteous.

He was the first to leave and Maggie found her mother staring at her—well, staring right through her, actually.

'What?' she queried.

'Nothing,' her mother replied absently.

'What did you think of him?' The question came out before Maggie could guard against it and she bit her lip.

'They could be two of a kind.'

Maggie's eyes widened. 'Jack and Dad? That's exactly what I thought in the beginning!'

'Yes, well…' Belle seemed to come to a decision, and she imparted some surprising news to Maggie. Her father had bid successfully on three cattle stations and for the next few months they would be spending most of their time on them in Central Queensland.

'That's quite a coup,' Maggie said dazedly.

Belle agreed. 'Will you come with us? We'd love to have you.'

'No. No… I'm fine here.' But would she be, she wondered, without her mother's moral support?

'Of course I'll come and see you frequently, darling,' Belle assured her, 'and I'll only ever be a phone call and a short flight away.'

It wasn't until months later that Maggie realized what a clever strategy of her mother's this was…

Three months went by and at last Maggie started to show some signs of her pregnancy.

They went surprisingly swiftly, those months. She made all the difficult explanations—much less difficult than the ones to her parents and Jack, but not easy either. It was one thing to announce you were pregnant and to produce a partner even if he wasn't a husband, quite another to have to explain you were doing it on your own.

Her boss was clearly concerned for her, but he did

agree it made no difference to her work and she could continue for as long as she wanted to.

'You have a real flair for it, Maggie,' he said to her. 'A born natural, you are.' Then he frowned and seemed about to say more, but he obviously changed his mind.

Tim Mitchell was the hardest of all to tell. He was horrified, he was mystified and he offered to marry her himself there and then.

She thanked him with real gratitude, but declined. And she gradually withdrew herself from the crowd they both moved in.

'You don't have to do that, Maggie,' Tim said reproachfully. 'You need friends at least!'

'Yes, but I'm a different person now. I guess I have different priorities. Tim…' she hesitated but knew she had to do it '…I'm a lost cause, but there's got to be the *right* girl for you out there and you should forget about me—like that, anyway.' She stopped rather painfully as her words raised echoes in her mind she'd rather forget. But after that, she always found an excuse not to see Tim.

The one person apart from her family she couldn't seem to withdraw from was Jack.

He came to see her frequently in those months, although he never repeated his offer of marriage. It puzzled her that he should do this—at least as frequently as he did. It made it harder for her because of all the memories it brought back, but every time she thought of refusing to see him, she also thought of her promise never to separate him from his child.

She knew that she *could* never do that and, not only because he simply wouldn't have it, but also because he'd let her glimpse the pain and trauma of being abandoned by your natural parents.

She told herself that it was going to be a fact of her life from now on, his platonic presence in it, and she might as well get used to it. And it was platonic. He didn't try to touch her; he didn't refer to Cape Gloucester.

It was as if the desire he'd once felt for her had been turned off at the main switch and that caused her a lot of soul-searching. Had it been *such* a light-hearted affair for him? Had he achieved his revenge with spectacular success? Was there another woman in his life now? Was he turned off by pregnancy?

Perhaps I should check that out with Aunt Elena, she thought once, with dry humour.

The same couldn't be said for her. Yes, she'd suffered a couple of months of numbness after leaving him. In contrast now she was visited acutely at times by cameos from their past, like the one when they'd dragged an inflatable mattress out onto the veranda under a full, golden moon...

'We could be anywhere,' she said dreamily as they lay side by side on a cool linen sheet and the dusky pink pillows from his bed. 'On a raft up the Nile.'

'What made you think of that?'

'Well, you can hear the water, it is a wooden floor. Gloucester Island could be a pyramid sailing past.' She turned on her front and propped her chin on her hands so she could watch him. 'Have you ever been up the Nile?'

'Yes, I have.' He had one arm bent behind his head and he cupped her shoulder with his free hand and slid his finger beneath the broad lacy strap of her sleepwear. 'Have you?'

'Mmm… With my parents when I was sixteen. I loved it. Sadly, however, the whole experience was so momentous, I made myself sick.'

A smile flickered across his lips. 'That could have been the Egyptian version of Delhi belly.'

She bent her knees and crossed her ankles in the air. 'I think Africa would suit you,' she told him reflectively, 'or would have in times gone past.'

'I do remind you of Dr Livingstone? How?' he queried amusedly.

'No. But maybe Denys Finch-Hatton. I've seen his grave in the Ngong Hills, you know.'

'Same trip?'

She nodded. 'And Karen Blixen's house. It's preserved in her memory. The Danish government gave it to the Kenyan government on independence. She's a bit of a hero of mine.'

He turned his head towards her. 'Are you trying to tell me I'm a disappointment to you because I'm no Denys Finch-Hatton?' he queried gravely.

She denied this seriously. 'Not at all.'

'You did say something about taking me for a more physical guy.'

Maggie curled her toes. 'I just got that impression—well, yes, it presented itself to me in the form of hunting wild animals, crewing racing yachts et cetera, but translated it seemed to me that you liked to test yourself to the limit.'

He was silent for an age, just stroking her shoulder, then, 'In lots of ways I do—and did. When I started out, using the bank's money, not mine, I took some huge gambles. I often had to strain every nerve just to keep my head above water.'

'Did you enjoy that?'

He grinned fleetingly. 'There were times when I was scared to death, but on the whole, I guess I did.'

'So I was right about you all along,' she said with deep satisfaction.

'Wise as well as beautiful…' He drew the strap of her top down. 'Striking as this outfit is, I've got the feeling it's going to get in my way.'

Maggie flipped over onto her back and sat upright. 'This outfit' was a camisole pyjama top in topaz silk edged with ivory lace and a matching pair of boxer shorts.

'That could be remedied.' She slipped the top off over her head.

He watched her as she sat straight-backed with her legs crossed, like a naked ivory statue in the moonlight, slim, beautifully curved, grave, young and gorgeous. Her hair was tied up loosely with wavy tendrils escaping down her neck.

He sat up abruptly. 'If we changed the location slightly, moved this raft east across the desert sands, say, I could be the Sheik of Araby and you could be a candidate for my harem.'

Maggie's lashes fluttered and she turned to him with an incredulous look, but a little pulse beating rather rapidly at the base of her throat.

'Jack! That's very—fanciful.'

He grimaced. 'Surprised you?'

'Uh—' she licked her lips '—yes.'

He shook his head wryly. 'I've surprised myself, but that's how you make me feel at this moment and you were the one who put us in another spot in the first place.'

She thought for a moment, then bowed her head. 'Do I qualify?'

'Oh, yes, fiery little one,' he drawled. 'You do.'

'Fiery?' She lifted her head.

He touched one nipple, then the other, then he trailed his fingers down her spine towards her bottom. 'Fiery, delicious, peachy—definitely peachy. I knew I was right about that even if I couldn't understand it at the time.'

'Right?' She looked confused. 'What do you mean?'

He laughed softly. 'Don't worry about it. Come here.'

She moved into his arms and not much later he made exquisite love to her in the moonlight, on their raft anchored in the sands of Araby.

Two things Jack touched on during his visits were rather surprising. His latest development project, a retirement village, and the property he'd bought.

'Not the one with a shed hijacked to hide some vintage vehicles, the one I locked us into?' she said, her eyes wide with surprise as she unconsciously repeated how he'd described it the last time it had been mentioned between them. 'I happen to know it's been sold to a company, Hanson Limited, or something like that.'

'It's one of my companies.'

It was a Sunday morning and he'd arrived just as she was starting a late breakfast. He wore a navy tracksuit and running shoes, his hair was windblown and he was glowing with vim and vigour.

'Good,' he added as he sat down at her breakfast table. 'I'm starving.'

'What have you been doing?' Maggie asked as she got out more plates and cutlery.

'A two-mile jog down Main Beach.'

'Then you might need something more substantial.. like steak and eggs.' She looked at him humorously.

He scanned the table. There was yoghurt and fruit, rolls and jam and, striking a slightly discordant note, a steaming bowl of chicken noodle soup.

He eyed it. 'Going for oriental cuisine, Maggie?'

She shrugged. 'I just get this incredible craving for chicken noodle soup. It can happen to me at any time of the day or night.'

'Out of a packet?'

'Oh, no. I make it myself so I can keep the level of salt down and there are no preservatives. I'm taking very good care of your unborn baby, Jack.'

He laughed. 'I wasn't suggesting otherwise. Well, don't let it get cold, I'll look after myself.'

'There's some leg ham and a nice piece of Cheddar in the fridge.' Maggie lifted a spoonful of soup to her mouth and blew on it gently. 'Help yourself if you like.'

He raised a wry eyebrow. 'A continental breakfast? I will, thanks.'

'So you bought it after all,' she said when he'd assembled a much larger breakfast and was tucking into it.

'Mmm… I thought you might be interested. Maisie said you had some good ideas for the house.'

'I'm sure you could afford to pull it down and start again.'

'I know you may still cherish the opinion that I delight in destroying landscapes and pulling things down to put up new ones, but in this case I don't,' he said mildly. 'That house has a lot of character and potential.'

Maggie drank her soup, having had the wind somewhat taken out of her sails. Nor was it that that she had against Jack McKinnon any longer, she reminded herself. It was the fact that he could arrive uninvited at her breakfast table, make himself completely at home—well, she had suggested that, but all the same—and, treacherously, it reminded her of all the breakfasts they'd shared at Cape Gloucester.

One particularly came to mind...

'What will we do today?'

He eyed her seriously. They'd had an early morning swim and she wore her pink bikini with her sarong knotted between her breasts. They were drinking coffee at the breakfast bar.

'Nothing,' he said.

'Nothing?' She wrinkled her nose at him. 'How idle!'

'I didn't plan to be completely idle. Perhaps decadent would be a better word for it—starting now.' He put his mug down and carefully untied the knot between her breasts to release her sarong, then he reached round and undid her bikini top.

Maggie looked downwards, entranced and feeling her heart start to beat heavily at the sight of his lean brown hands on her breasts.

'It doesn't feel decadent to me,' she said softly and bit her lip as her nipples flowered and a wash of sensuousness ran through her body.

'Actually—' he looked up briefly '—I can't think of anything more lovely and fresh and entirely the opposite from decadent than you, Ms Trent.'

'So?' Maggie queried with difficulty.

'I was referring to the time of day, that's all. Eight o'clock in the morning is not renowned for its romantic properties. Moonlit evenings, starry, starry nights, dawn, perhaps?' He looked into her eyes and shook his head. 'However…'

She put her hands on his shoulders and rested her forehead against his. 'Eight o'clock in the morning feels very romantic to me.'

He lifted her off her stool to sit across his lap, and slid his hands beneath her bikini bottom to cup her hips. 'You are a siren, you know,' he said against the corner of her mouth.

'Not Delilah?'

'Her too… Come to bed.'

She came out of her reverie feeling hot and cold, aroused and with her senses clamouring for that touch on her body again as she remembered the slow, perfectly lovely way he'd made love to her despite it being eight o'clock in the morning.

I thought I had it all sorted out, she reflected bitterly. I was no one's hostage; I was this independent, mature—recently matured but all the same—person in charge of my own destiny. So why can't I forget Cape Gloucester and all the things he did to me?

'I did have some ideas,' she said abruptly, anything to banish those images from her mind. 'But they wouldn't—' she wrinkled her nose as she forced herself to concentrate '—come cheap.'

'Spoken like a true Trent,' he murmured, and

grinned at her expression. 'That's fine with me. If I'm going to do it I want to do it properly. Tell me your thoughts.'

She did. And she couldn't fight the quickening of interest she felt.

CHAPTER SEVEN

THE next time Jack came to see Maggie, as usual unannounced, he dumped a heap of blueprints on her coffee-table.

'What on earth…?' She stared at him.

'I'm planning a retirement village. I do not want it to resemble a bloody chicken coop, but it has to stay affordable. What do you think of these?'

She took her time as she paged through the designs. 'Ghastly,' she pronounced at last. 'They're so poky!'

'That's what I told the architect. He's withdrawn from the project. On the other hand, they are retirement homes, not vast mansions.'

Maggie pulled some cushions behind her back, which ached occasionally nowadays, and considered the matter. 'I think it would be a help if they were more open plan. Separate bedrooms, yes, but not separate boxy little kitchens, dining rooms and lounges, so you got a more spacious feel even if it isn't necessarily so.'

He waited alertly as she thought some more.

'And since they don't have gardens—'

'Retirees are generally longing to get away from being slaves to lawnmowers and the like,' he put in.

'Perhaps,' she conceded, 'but a decent veranda so they can grow some nice pot plants and herbs if they want to would be…would be a priority of mine.'

'There are going to be plenty of landscaped gardens,' he murmured. 'All taken care of for them.'

'It's not the same as suddenly being cut off from growing anything of your *own*,' she countered. 'In fact, if I were planning a retirement village, I'd set aside a section where those interested could have their own little plots to grow their own vegetables or whatever they liked.'

'You are a gardening fanatic, Maggie,' he pointed out and glanced at the riot of colour outside.

She shrugged. 'Those are my ideas!'

'OK. I'll come back to you on it.'

'Why me?' she asked.

'I think you might have a feel for these things which could be helpful to me, Ms Trent. I've never done a retirement village before. I've been more concerned with kids and families.'

'Oh.'

He looked amused. 'If you feel like doing some designing, some doodles even, I'd be very appreciative.'

Maggie blinked, but she allowed the matter to drop.

For some reason, she'd recently begun to feel as if she'd walked into a brick wall and nothing was of more than passing interest to her.

Or rather, one reason for it was loud and clear. Added to her memories, added to her growing desire to drop all her defences and say simply to Jack, Marry me, please, I need you and I can't do this on my own, was her growing curiosity about other women in his life. It haunted her. There were times when it made her hate him and be prickly and uncommunicative with him. It sapped her energy. It was entirely unreasonable, she tried to tell herself.

You wouldn't marry him when the offer was open. Perhaps the best thing for you *is* to hate him…

On the other hand, when she wasn't being cross and out of sorts with him, she had to admit that his presence in her life was a bit like a rock she was coming to rely on.

What a mess you are, Maggie, she thought frequently.

She was five and a half months pregnant when he called in one chilly evening after dinner time.

They talked about nothing very much for a while, then he fell silent as his grey gaze flickered over her. She wore a loose ivory wool sweater over dark green tartan stretch pants. The sleeves of the sweater were a fraction too long for her and sometimes she folded them back, but they always unrolled.

Was it that, he wondered, that gave her a waif-like air? The exposure of her fragile wrists? Her loose hair tucked behind her ears? Her cream flat shoes that reminded him of ballet shoes?

Or her secretive eyes?

Grave and secretive now, when they'd been like windows of her soul only a few months ago. Capable of teasing him, querying him or laughing at him in a swift green glance, expressing honest desire. Expressing joy or, of course, sparkling with anger. But that had been longer ago, the anger, and what crazy voice in him told him he'd prefer that to this secretiveness?

'How are you feeling?' he asked abruptly.

'Fine,' she replied automatically.

'No, tell me.' He'd come straight from a business dinner and hadn't discarded his jacket, although he'd loosened his tie.

Maggie pushed a cushion behind the small of her

back. 'Apart from a bit of backache I do feel fine. The morning—afternoon sickness has gone and I'm told this middle trimester, before you get too heavy and slow, is when you should really glow.' She grimaced.

'But you're not glowing, are you?' he said quietly.

She shrugged and stood up suddenly. 'According to my doctor every pregnancy can be different. Would you like a cup of tea? Or a drink? I'm dying for a cuppa.'

'Thanks, I'll have one too.'

She turned away, but not before he noted some differences in her figure. Her wrists might look fragile, but those high, firm little gymnast's breasts were ripening and her waist was no longer reed-slim...

When she brought the tea tray back, he studied it rather than her figure.

He knew she liked Earl Grey tea so he wasn't surprised at the subtle fragrance of citrus oil of Bergamot that rose above the lovely china cups as she poured boiling water into them.

He knew she drank hers black and sugarless, but she hadn't forgotten that he took milk. He knew she always deposited the tea bags into an antique silver dish decorated with griffins rampant.

'All the same, why is that, do you think?' he queried as he accepted his cup and took a shortbread biscuit from the salver she offered.

'Why is what?'

'Is it the strain of being a single mother? Is that why you're not glowing, since there aren't any other problems?' he said deliberately.

She sat down and tucked her legs up. 'You'd be the last person I'd confess that to—if it were true.'

'In case I repeated my offer of marriage? I'm not.'

She pushed her sleeves back and wrapped her hands around her cup. 'No, it wouldn't make any difference. It's still no one's fault but my own that I find myself a bit daunted at times, but especially not yours, that's why I wouldn't admit it to you.' She hesitated. 'It's probably only because it's such new territory and many a new mum might feel a bit daunted anyway.'

'Have you made any preparations for the baby?'

A glint of humour beamed his way. 'Jack, whenever my mother comes to visit me, which is frequently, we do nothing else. That's not quite true—we go to the movies, concerts and so on and every few weeks she insists I spend a weekend on the cattle stations with them. But this baby will have everything that opens and shuts; more clothes than any single baby could wear, many of them exquisitely hand stitched. She loves doing that kind of delicate sewing.'

'OK.' He finished his tea and thought for a bit. 'What about your other social life?'

She wrinkled her nose. 'What social life?'

'Well, girlfriends, then?'

Maggie sighed unexpectedly. 'One or two, but I think I may have been a bit—I don't know—I think I may have given off pretty strong vibes that I would rather be alone.'

'And Tim Mitchell?'

She flinched.

'Did he drop you like the proverbial hot potato?'

'Oh, no. He offered to marry me.'

'I hope you turned him down flat,' he said and was rewarded by a definitely hostile green glance.

'Tim would make a fine husband,' she said tersely.

'Come on, Maggie,' he drawled, knowing full well he was out to hurt and anger her further, as if he had the devil himself riding him, 'that would have been a recipe for disaster. At least you loved going to bed with me.'

'Don't say—'

'Another word? Why not? It's true. You certainly made love to me as if you loved every minute of it. You tracked me down where no outsider has ever been able to find me to do so, come to that,' he said lazily, then added, 'And all the while you had Tim Mitchell virtually sitting in your lap.'

Maggie gasped. 'That's…that's—'

But he broke in before she could go on. 'If you're contemplating a loveless marriage to anyone, Maggie, I fail to see what Tim Mitchell has over me. Then again, I did think that's what you were expressly holding out against.'

'I am. If you'd allowed me to finish you would have heard me say that Tim would make a fine husband for the right person who was not *me*.'

'Bravo,' he applauded. 'I'm all in favour of sticking to your guns. Did that ring a bell with you, though?'

'It gave me a distinct sense of *déjà vu*,' she replied through her teeth. 'Why are you being so—horrible?'

He shrugged. 'I thought you needed taking out of yourself a bit.' He ignored her incredulous expression. 'How's the job going?'

Maggie opened her mouth to dispose of this query summarily, but something stopped her. Did she need taking out of herself? Was she floundering in a slough of despond?

'I'm giving it up in a fortnight.' She sniffed suddenly. 'I seem to have lost my edge. It's become a bit of a chore rather than a pleasure. Besides which…' she looked down at herself ruefully '…I've got the feeling I'm about to burst out all over and driving around a lot and getting in and out of cars may not be too comfortable.'

He smiled, and it was almost as if he'd gone from tiger mode to gentle mode in the blink of an eye. 'You could be right. How about working from home? For me, I mean, or as an associate?'

Maggie stared at him.

'I adapted the retirement village to your ideas, but now I need an interior decorator.' He paused and looked around. 'You have some wonderful ideas and taste.'

Maggie stared at him with her lips parted this time.

'You seem to have pretty strong convictions about retirement homes,' he said into the silence with a tinge of irony.

'Are you furnishing them?' she queried.

'Not all of them. There are several levels of accommodation. The ones I will be furnishing are for single occupants, widows and widowers mostly, I guess. I'd like them to be—cheerful and comfortable. But even the ones I don't furnish will need colour schemes, carpets, curtains, kitchen and bathroom finishes, et cetera.'

'And…' she licked her lips '…you…you think I could do all that from home?'

'I don't see why not. Of course you can check out the site as often as you like, but Maisie could organize all the samples—fabrics, carpet, paint—to be sent here.'

She stared at him again, transfixed.

He waited for a moment, then added, 'I've also set aside some land that can be divided into plots for keen gardeners.'

Why that did it, she wasn't sure, but all of a sudden, although it was a huge project, it beckoned her in a way that lifted her spirits immediately.

She opened her mouth to say the first thing that popped into her mind—*What a pity you don't love me, Jack*—but at the last moment she amended it to, 'Why are you doing this?'

'I told you. Your welfare is important to me, as well as the kid's.'

She fell asleep with tears on her cheeks that night because that unbidden, out-of-context thought—*what a pity you don't love me, Jack*—had revealed to her that she still hungered for his love; perhaps she always would. Why it had popped into her mind, she wasn't sure. Because he'd taken her advice to heart on garden plots for retirees? That didn't make much sense. Or did it? Could they become quite a team in every respect but the one that mattered most and it broke her heart to think of it?

Her life changed, her outlook in most respects changed from then on, however. During the last few months of her pregnancy she became very busy and found it fulfilling. She did pop out in some directions, but she did also glow, at times, at last.

She also got closer to Jack and the McKinnon empire. She accepted an advisory position on his board, although she demurred at first on the grounds of the speculation it might produce along the lines of whose baby she was carrying.

'That's no one's business but our own, Maggie,' he said decidedly. 'Anyway, no one knows of our connection. I haven't told anyone.'

'Not even Maisie?'

'Not even Maisie, although she may suspect, but she's the soul of discretion. Have you told anyone?'

'Who the father is? No.'

They eyed each other until he said, 'Well, then? It could be the start of a new, more suitable career for you as a single mother.'

Maggie opened her mouth, but, much as she would have loved to refute this for reasons not at all clear to her, she couldn't deny it was something she should give thought to.

'You could be right,' she said eventually.

She got to know his sub-penthouse, which was where he did his business entertaining. It was elegant but restrained and she got the feeling that if he felt really at home anywhere, it was Cape Gloucester.

She experienced the dynamic businessman he was at firsthand and knew that she and her mother had been right: he could be as arrogant and ruthless as her father, but he did temper it so that all his employees were devoted to him and his partners in any ventures respected him highly.

Sylvia came to see her out of the blue one day.

'I got Jack's permission to do this,' she said as she stood on the doorstep.

Still blinking with surprise, Maggie said, 'You

didn't need his permission! Uh—come in. I didn't know you knew…'

'I didn't until a couple of days ago when I came up to tell him some news of my own. I do find,' Sylvia said wryly when they were settled in the lounge, 'that it's not a good idea to cross Jack these days. Actually, it never was, because even as a kid he had an infuriating habit of being right about most things.'

'I know the kind.' Maggie looked heavenwards.

'I suppose you do. You got sandwiched between two such men, didn't you?'

The reference to her father chilled Maggie a little and perhaps Sylvia sensed it because she went on in a sudden rush. 'I was as much to blame as your father was. I knew he was married. I should never have got involved.'

Maggie thawed, she couldn't help it, but she also said honestly, 'I wondered about that. Still, these things happen, I guess.'

'Something else has happened to me. I've fallen in love again when I thought it could never happen to me.'

'Not a married man?'

'Not a married man, but he will be married to me shortly.'

On an impulse Maggie got up and crossed over to Sylvia to hug her with some difficulty that caused them both to laugh.

'I'm so happy for you,' Maggie said, with a genuine feeling of warmth.

'Would there be—any possibility your mother and father have—have…?' Sylvia hesitated.

'Got together again?' Maggie supplied. 'Yes! They have and it's wonderful to see.'

Sylvia breathed deeply. 'That's an enormous relief. But has he forgiven you for Jack, and this?'

'This?' Maggie patted her stomach affectionately. 'He's putting a good face on it. I don't think they'll ever be friends, but somehow or other I made them see that they had to be civilized at least. Not that they've met yet.'

'Maggie, why won't you marry Jack?'

'Sylvia…' Maggie paused and searched Sylvia's blue eyes '…you could be the one person who knows how hard it is to pin the real Jack McKinnon down. I think there's a core in him that will always shy away…' she stopped to think carefully '…from any true attachment and it goes right back to being put up for adoption as a baby.'

Sylvia heaved a sigh. 'Even under a loving adoption arrangement, it can be like a thorn in your flesh or you can secretly hold the belief that your mother was this wonderful, wonderful person who is always tied to you by an invisible string. That's the path I opted for. Jack went the other way. You could be right but—'

'The thing is,' Maggie interrupted quietly, 'I'm an all-or-nothing kind of person.' She raised her eyebrows. 'In lots of respects I've come to see I might be a chip off the old block, after all.'

'He, Jack, I mean—'

Again Maggie interrupted. 'He's been wonderful in lots of ways.'

'He was wonderful to me when I—when your father—without Jack to pick up the pieces, I don't know where I'd be.'

'Yes, he is rather good at picking up the pieces, isn't he?' Maggie said slowly.

Sylvia looked awkward. 'I didn't mean you.'

Maggie grimaced and decided to change the subject completely. 'Tell me about your new man? And would you like to see the nursery?'

'Well, well, kiddo.' Maggie patted her stomach after Sylvia had left—she'd taken to talking to her baby ever since she'd come out of her slough of despond. 'That was your aunt. Come to think of it, that's yet another difficult situation resolved. Which only leaves us but, hey, between the two of us we can conquer anything!'

A couple of days later, she got an even greater surprise.

Jack held a dinner party to celebrate the retirement village foundations being dug.

Actually, it was Maisie who organized it all down to the caterers, the flowers and guest list.

Maggie received her invitation in the mail. Jack was overseas until the afternoon of the dinner, but she didn't RSVP until the last moment. She was in two minds.

Then she thought, What the heck? She was part of the team and although, at eight months, sitting for any length of time was uncomfortable, she felt absolutely fine.

She also went out of her way to look absolutely fine. She chose a long French navy dress in a silk georgette that, despite being a maternity dress, was the essence of chic. It was round-necked, sleeveless and spring-like in tune with the new season. The fine pintucking on the bodice was stitched with silver thread.

She got her hair and her nails done; her tawny hair was loose and lightly curled so that it looked gorgeously windswept as only an expert hairdresser could achieve.

Her shoes were a complete folly, she knew—high, strappy silver sandals she couldn't have resisted if she'd tried. She covered the few patches of pregnancy pigment on her cheeks with a glowing foundation and her lipstick matched her nail polish.

She stared at herself in her beautiful rosewood cheval-mirror and addressed her unborn child again…

'You couldn't say we were *hugely* pregnant, honey-child. I've been very careful dietary-wise and I've been pretty active. Incidentally, *you're* pretty active these days, a right little gymnast! But I am more, well, rounded, even in the less obvious areas, although it doesn't seem to look too bad. Not tonight anyway.'

She turned away from the mirror ruefully and swept her silver mesh purse off the bed.

Maisie was more positive about it when she met Maggie at the door of the sub-penthouse.

'Maggie,' she said affectionately—they'd become good friends, 'you look fantastic!'

'I second that.' Jack loomed up behind Maisie and Maggie took an unexpected little breath.

She hadn't seen him for a week, but it was more than that. He wore a dinner suit and the beautifully tailored black suit and white shirt highlighted his tall, strong lines and broad shoulders. It shot through her mind that she loved him however he looked.

Windblown and with blue shadows on his jaw,

wearing an old football jersey with the sleeves cut off as he'd often been at Cape Gloucester—but this Jack was electrifying.

She swallowed something in her throat. 'Thanks, you two! You sure know how to make a very pregnant lady feel better.'

It was a buffet dinner for about twenty people and because it was a calm, warm night there were tables set out on the veranda high above Runaway Bay and overlooking the Broadwater and the ocean beyond.

The food was inspired and fine wine flowed although Maggie didn't partake of the wine and she ate sparingly. But the company was pleasant, she knew everyone and she enjoyed herself.

All the same, she attempted to leave a little early. She was making her explanations to Maisie when Jack's hand closed round her wrist. 'Stay a bit longer,' he said quietly. 'It won't be long before the party breaks up. Then I can drive you home.'

'But I drove myself here,' she objected.

'Doesn't matter. You shouldn't be out and about on your own at this time of night.'

'That's true,' Maisie agreed.

'I am a little tired, though,' Maggie said and stifled a yawn.

'How about I settle you in the den where you can put your feet up and bring you a cuppa?' Maisie offered.

'Oh, thank you!' Maggie said gratefully. 'My shoes are killing me.'

Maggie had never seen the den and it brought a slight smile to her lips. There was definitely a nautical flavour to it.

There were gold-framed ships on the walls; there was a wonderful antique globe of the world and a polished brass sextant on the coffee-table. There were also deep, inviting buttoned leather armchairs…

'And this one,' said Maisie triumphantly as she pushed a lever on the side of the chair, 'is a recliner chair.'

'Just what I need!' Maggie slipped off her shoes and sank down into it gratefully.

'Tea's on the way!'

Maggie had her tea, then she stretched out in the chair, to find she couldn't keep her eyes open.

Half an hour later something woke her from the gentle slumber she'd fallen into. Her lashes lifted, and Jack was standing beside the chair looking down at her, Jack looking austere but divine with his streaky fair hair tamed tonight and that wonderful physique highlighted by his dinner suit.

Her lips parted as their gazes caught and held, then she struggled upright.

He held out his hand and helped her to her feet.

She opened her mouth to thank him, but the words died on her lips because he was studying her—in a way she knew well, a way that was anything but austere—from top to toe. The sleep-flushed curves of her face, the glorious disarray of her hair, her mouth and throat, her full, rich breasts beneath the fine navy georgette, the mound of his child…

His gaze was intent and heavy-lidded and the pressure of his fingers on hers grew.

He still wants me, Maggie thought chaotically as

her colour fluctuated and her breathing grew ragged. That's how he used to look at me before he made love to me, just like this… So that the power of his gaze was almost like having his hands on me.

Have I not been the only one to suffer from the unassuaged ache of being physically deprived of him? Not the only one plagued by so many memories of our lovemaking? she wondered wildly. But what does it mean? I was so sure that he'd stopped wanting me.

She was destined not to know what it meant. A phone rang softly on the desk.

He turned his head at last to look at it, a hard, irritable look, then as it rang on he shrugged and walked over to it.

'Maisie,' he growled down the line, 'what the hell—?' He stopped.

From then on he answered in monosyllables until he said, 'All right. Will you drive Maggie home?'

She looked a question at him as he put the phone down.

'Sylvia rang. Our mother is critically ill now and not likely to survive for more than a day or so.'

'I'm sorry,' she said quietly. 'Don't worry about me—but will you get a flight at this time of night?'

'No, and the earliest flights tomorrow are booked out so I'll drive. If I start off now, I'll get there early tomorrow morning, anyway. I'm sorry.'

'That's all right! Just—take care. On the road.'

'I will.' He picked up her hand. 'You take care too.'

The baby moved at that moment and she put her hand on her stomach with his over it.

He blinked as he felt the movement. 'How often does that happen?'

'Quite a lot nowadays.' A smile trembled on her lips. 'He or she loves doing cartwheels so we could have another gymnast on our hands.'

Maisie coughed discreetly from the doorway, and the moment was lost. 'Sylvia again,' she said apologetically.

For the next few days Maggie felt as if she were on cloud nine.

Don't equate wanting you with loving you and not being able to live without you, she warned herself, but it made no difference. The long months of unhappiness, of blaming herself for her situation, of feeling that she hadn't lived up to what he needed in a woman melted away behind her.

If he could still want her when she was eight months pregnant, maybe he always would? Had she been proud and foolish all that time?

But I didn't know, she thought dazedly. He hid it so well. Why?

This thought occurred to her as she was walking down a busy pavement in Southport on the way to her doctor. She didn't even notice the man who passed her, then turned round and came back to her.

Until he said, 'Hang on—don't I know you?'

Maggie blinked and stared at him uncomprehendingly.

'You weren't pregnant then and all you were wearing was a bra and jeans while you and Jack McKinnon were—supposedly, although I had my doubts—trying to get out of the roof of a shed.'

Maggie suffered a surge of sheer revulsion at the

hateful way the man's eyes gleamed, and recognition came to her. It was the journalist who'd been with the private detective when she and Jack had been locked in the shed.

When he put his hand on her arm to detain her, she wrenched it free. 'Go away,' she ordered and made a dash for her doctor's surgery only a few doors away.

She heaved a huge sigh of relief as she passed through the doors and no one followed her, although she supposed it was always possible he would hang around until she came out.

Maisie, she thought. I'll ring Maisie and ask her to pick me up. Maisie will know how to handle it.

She got out her mobile phone and did just that.

But the first question she asked Maisie was if she'd heard from Jack.

'I just got the call. Mrs McKinnon passed away this morning. I believe it was a blessed relief.'

'Oh, that's still so sad. Please pass on my deepest sympathy.' Maggie paused, then went on to explain her current situation.

'I'll come and get you,' Maisie said immediately. 'Just tell me where and stay put in your doctor's rooms.'

When Maggie ended the call, she looked around and discovered she was in the wrong corridor.

She turned back just as a little boy, looking gleefully over his shoulder at his mother who was in hot pursuit, raced towards her.

They collided.

The child fell over, but bounced up. Maggie, robbed of her usual agility, toppled over with one ankle twisted beneath her. She fell on her back and hit her head on the floor. She passed out like a light.

CHAPTER EIGHT

SHE swam up slowly out of a deep, dreamless sleep. She opened her eyes a couple of times, but it was too much of an effort to keep them open. The third time she did it, though, she moved her head slightly and something swam into her line of vision that caused her to keep them open—a crib.

She froze as jumbled, painful memories tumbled through her mind, some memories of labour and the enormous effort and concentration it had required, memories of all sorts of people attending to her and X-raying her, but no memories of a birth.

She clutched her stomach and found it flat but floppy rather than hard and round. She froze again and realized her deep sleep since then must have been sedative-assisted because someone had put her into a fresh nightgown and a crisply made bed in a strange room she'd never seen before. And someone had put a crib beside the bed.

She moved convulsively but found her lower limbs wouldn't move at all.. and Jack said quietly, 'Take it easy, Maggie.'

Her astonished gaze fell on him, sitting on a chair beside the crib. 'Jack!'

'Yes. How do you feel?'

'I have no idea.' She blinked rapidly. 'Is this—us?'

He looked briefly amused. 'A good way to put it. Uh—it says on the crib—Trent stroke McKinnon—

so I guess it must be.' He tilted the crib so Maggie could see into it.

There was a baby fast asleep in it.

'So it's all right? It's…*all right*?' she asked urgently.

'Fine. Quite perfect, in fact, so they tell me.'

Maggie fell back against the pillows with a gasp of relief. 'Girl or boy?'

'Boy. He's a little premature and he's spent a bit of time in a humidicrib but they reckon he's coping very well on his own.'

She studied the baby, not that she could see much more than the curve of a cheek, one tiny fist and a fuzz of brown hair. Then he moved and more of his features came into view—and Maggie held her breath. But with great seriousness, the infant Trent stroke McKinnon yawned, opened his hand, then slept on.

'He seems to be…very composed,' Maggie said in some confusion.

'Yeah.' Jack shoved a hand through his hair, then rubbed his unshaven jaw. 'A lot more composed than I feel.'

'How can that be so?' she queried seriously. 'After what he's been through?'

'You were the one who went through the worst.'

'I don't seem to remember a lot about it,' she confessed. 'Well, some parts of it, but it's all confused and fuzzy.'

'Just as well and not surprising—you had concussion on top of everything else.'

Jack paused, then reached for her hand. 'What happened was, you sprained your ankle when you fell, you have a bump on your head and they think you may have slipped a disc or done something to your back. Then you went into labour. Fortunately, Maisie arrived not long after it all happened and she was able to identify you and get your own doctor—they'd called out another doctor who has consulting rooms in the same building.'

'Why can't I move my legs?' she asked.

'You've had a couple of epidurals. The birth itself was quite straightforward so they chose not to intervene—seems this young man had decided not to muck around!' He smiled at her. 'But you were in a lot of pain from your back as well as your ankle so it was for your sake and it may take a while to wear off.'

She blinked dazedly. 'How long ago did this all happen?'

He looked at his watch. 'About eight hours ago. I got here just after he was born.' He smiled again and released her hand to stroke her hair for a moment. 'I've had my first cuddle.'

Maggie closed her eyes. 'Can I?' she said with absolute longing in her voice.

'Sure. Your parents are also here, incidentally. They went to have a cup of coffee.'

Maggie's lashes swept up. 'You—you and my father have met?'

He nodded. 'No fireworks, no hard words. We're all too concerned about you. And too taken with the baby.'

Maggie breathed very deeply. 'That's—I can't tell you how happy that makes me.'

He said nothing, just stroked her hair again.

'And my back?' she asked after a while.

'They're not sure. What with everything else going on—' he gestured ruefully '—they haven't been able to assess it properly. But they have taken X-rays. We're waiting on the results now. Your ankle just needs time.'

'Will you please give me my baby, Jack?' she begged. 'You see, I've been talking to it, to him,' she corrected herself, 'for weeks and weeks and I'm sure he can't understand why he hasn't heard my voice since he was born.'

'Of course.' He got up and picked Trent stroke McKinnon up gingerly. In the moment before he placed the bundle in Maggie's arms, he looked down at the child in a way that made Maggie catch her breath—with sheer pride and tenderness.

It shot through her mind that even if she never achieved a breakthrough to the real Jack McKinnon, this child would.

Then she accepted the bundle and her own attachment began. Her breasts tightened and she put a finger into her son's open palm and his tiny hand closed around it.

'Well, well, honey-child,' she breathed, 'we get to meet at last. How do you do? Oh, look,' she said to Jack, 'I think he's got your nose!'

Jack grimaced and felt his nose. 'If there's anyone he looks like,' he said ruefully, 'it's a Trent.'

They laughed together—and that was how her parents found them.

But when the injections wore off a couple of hours later, Maggie was once again in great pain, although at least the cause of it had been diagnosed. She'd broken a transverse process, a small bone running off the spine, in her lower back.

It would heal, she was told, of its own accord, but

many movements would be painful for her until it did so. All they could do was manage the pain for her until it became bearable, in about a week they estimated, but even then it would probably be quite a few weeks before she regained full mobility.

Unfortunately, they told her, all this would interfere with her ability to breast-feed her baby.

'No, it won't,' she said.

'Maggie,' her mother began.

'Mum, there has to be a way. Dad—' she turned her head to her father '—why don't you take Jack out for a drink while we work this out? He looks as if he could do with it.'

'Maggie,' David Trent warned, 'darling, it's not the end of the world if you can't breast-feed and it's just as important for the baby for you to recover well and quickly.'

'I will,' she promised, 'but I will also do this, *somehow.*'

It occurred to her a moment later that she never, ever thought she'd see what she saw then—her father and Jack exchange identical helpless glances.

Belle also saw it and she exchanged a laughing glance with Maggie before she shooed both men out. Then she sobered and turned back to her daughter. 'How?'

'I've read a lot about it and there's great support for breast-feeding mums. What we need is an expert, but I don't see why my milk can't be expressed for the next few days so I don't lose it, until I come off the painkillers—and I intend to do that as soon as possible.'

'But what about the baby?'

'We need to find someone with loads of milk who

wouldn't mind suckling him so he gets the hang of it, and they will have to feed him a supplement. Mum, please help me here,' Maggie said urgently, then looked exhausted. 'I want to do this!'

Belle eyed her daughter, then sighed. 'All right. All right.'

It was a traumatic and painful week for Maggie. Expressing breast milk might sound fine in theory, but in practice it could be excruciating. Transverse processes might be little bones, but they hurt like the devil when you broke them.

On the plus side, however, Bev Janson, who'd had her third baby the same day as Maggie's, had more milk than she knew what to do with and was grateful for the relief she gained from feeding another baby. Not only that, she and Maggie became firm friends.

And Trent stroke McKinnon throve through it all.

Then came the day when Maggie could sit up properly and she was given the go-ahead to feed her baby herself.

Her sense of triumph was huge. So was her joy.

'See?' she said to Jack. 'I knew there had to be a way.'

'Maggie…' He stopped, then shook his head at her. 'You're a bloody marvel. I don't think I've ever seen such guts.'

'The doctor said I could probably go home in three or four days.'

He hesitated. 'Have you had any thoughts about that?'

'No!' She grimaced. 'Too much on my mind.'

'We have.'

She eyed him. Apart from a couple of days when

he'd gone south for his mother's funeral, he'd spent time with her every day.

He'd taken the nursing staff by storm.

He'd brought her a DVD machine and lots of movies, including all the Harry Potter movies; he'd brought her books. He'd sent Bev a magnificent floral tribute and got friendly with her husband. On discovering the Jansons would dearly love to move into a bigger house than the one they were renting but couldn't afford to, he'd organized one at the same rent for them on one of his estates.

But he'd said nothing about marriage, although, when he was with her in her painful times, Maggie could have been forgiven for thinking he cared deeply about her.

Now, it was a Sunday, he wore jeans, deck shoes and a white polo T-shirt. He looked casual, big and…

Maggie paused in her summary of him. And what…?

'We have?' she repeated suspiciously. 'Who are we?'

'Your parents and I. We came to the conclusion it would be a good idea if you moved in with me.'

'Jack—'

'I have so much space and it's all on one level whereas your house is double-storeyed—'

'I know that!'

He half smiled. 'Then you'll agree that since you'll need a wheelchair for a while it makes sense not to have stairs to negotiate.'

She was silent as she stared at him fixedly.

'Your mother has offered to stay with us for as long as you need her,' he went on. 'There's also a gymnasium in the building and a swimming pool. Your doctors have recommended a programme of exercise under a physiotherapist's care to get your back and your ankle strong again.'

'I see,' she said at last.

'What do you see, Maggie?' he asked with his lips quirking.

'Something I never thought I would live to see,' she said. 'You and my parents ganging up on me.'

He opened his mouth to reply, but a nurse walked in with their baby in her arms. 'Feed time! Now listen up, you two.' She gave the baby to Maggie. 'We, the nursing staff, have decided it's about time this baby got a name. You can't go on calling him Trent stroke McKinnon for the rest of his life!'

'How about,' Jack suggested, 'Trent McKinnon?'

'Trent McKinnon,' Maggie said slowly. 'Do you approve, sweetheart?' she asked the baby.

Their child wrinkled his face and began to wave his fists, a prelude, Maggie was coming to know well, to a very vocal infant conniption. 'Call me what you like; just feed me!' Maggie said rapidly and started to unbutton her nightgown.

They all laughed.

'Yes, I like that,' she added, 'but he needs a middle name—can be very helpful in certain circumstances, kiddo! So, let's make it Trent Jack McKinnon.'

'Agreed.' Jack got up and kissed her briefly. 'I've got to go, but I'll be back this evening. Shall I set it all up?'

Maggie looked up from her baby with a tinge of confusion, then she nodded helplessly and turned her concentration back to Trent Jack McKinnon.

It all went according to plan.

Maggie grew stronger and used the motorized

wheelchair less and less, but it was still invaluable by
the time Trent was two months old because it allowed
her to do everything for him without placing the burden of his weight on her back and ankle.

One of the bedrooms in the sub-penthouse had been
converted to his nursery cum her bedroom and, with
his flair for good design, Jack had had all the surfaces,
change table and so on, made to a height Maggie
could cope with sitting down.

He'd also taken advantage of her mother's presence
to catch up with business trips he'd put on hold while
Maggie had been in hospital. So they hadn't seen a
great deal of him—for which Maggie had been curiously grateful.

She tried desperately to analyze not only her feelings, but the whole situation as her strength returned,
but all she could come up with was the fact that she
only seemed to be able to take each day as it came
with a sense of what will be will be.

Then her mother decided to go back to the cattle
stations. She left the day Jack was due to return after
a week in New Zealand.

For some reason, although Maggie was perfectly
confident with Trent now, although she experienced
no pain now and wasn't afraid to be left alone, the
quiet, empty apartment acted as a catalyst for her.

She started to think of the future. She started to
question Jack's feelings for her, and hers for him.

There had been no repeat of what had taken place
in the den a few nights before Trent was born, but
that wasn't so surprising in the circumstances, and she
might have been partly responsible for it anyway. She
had been preoccupied with her baby and getting herself fit again for him. Jack, apparently, had had a lot

of work to catch up on. And her mother had been with them all the time.

Yet, lately, little things about him had started to catch her unawares.

She'd been talking to him over breakfast one morning when she'd found herself breaking off and watching the way he was drumming his fingers on the table. It was a habit she'd first noticed at Cape Gloucester and it suddenly reminded her of his fingers on her skin, exploring, tantalizing her until she was weak with desire…

She'd had to get up without finishing what she was saying on the pretext of hearing Trent.

He'd come back from one trip, but had only been able to spend half an hour with them before going off to a meeting. She'd unpacked his bag for him and she'd suddenly buried her face in one of his unlaundered shirts, feeling a little dizzy with longing for his tall, strong body on hers.

So not a lot has changed there, she thought, while she waited for Jack to come back from New Zealand. I still don't know where he stands, though, but I do know he's been wonderful in every other way.

She was sitting on her bed as she thought these thoughts, with Trent lying beside her obviously deeply interested in his teddy bear.

She leant over and tickled him under the chin. He made a trilling little sound, then grabbed her hand and started to nuzzle it.

'But in the end, honey-child,' she said to him, 'what it boils down to is this—if your mama thought only of herself in times gone by, that has to change. OK, I know! You're hungry.'

*   *   *

Jack got home just after Maggie had given Trent his six p.m. feed and was settling him.

She was still in the nursery when she heard him arrive and called out to him. 'In here, Jack!'

He came through a few minutes later looking rather tired. He wore khaki trousers and a round-necked T-shirt under a tweed sports jacket.

'A busy trip?' she queried.

'Yep.' He stretched. 'How's my son and heir?'

'He's fine. He was talking to his teddy bear today. Jack.' Maggie hesitated, then knew there was only one way to do what she had to do and that was to plunge right in. 'This is a very proper baby.'

Jack stared at his now-sleeping son for a long moment, then sat down on the end of her bed. 'I never thought he was a porcelain doll.'

'No. I mean, he's very well organized. He does everything by the book.'

Jack frowned. 'He's only eight weeks old. How can you say that?'

Maggie was still sitting in her wheelchair, attractively dressed in slim white trousers and a floral seersucker jacket trimmed with green. Her dark gold hair was tied back with a scrunchie; her green eyes were clear and free of pain.

'I'll tell you. He adapted himself to a four-hourly schedule right from the start under extremely difficult circumstances. He burps beautifully and he mostly sleeps between feeds just as the book says he should. He has one wakeful period, after his two p.m. feed, where he'll accept conversation and he quite appreciates being carried around for a bit. He now sleeps through the eight hours from ten p.m. to six a.m.'

'Is there anything he doesn't do by the book?' Jack asked with a grin. 'He sounds almost too good to be true.'

Maggie considered. 'He hates having his hair washed. He gets extremely upset, but even that isn't going against the book exactly. They do warn that some babies hate it.'

'Screams blue murder?'

'Yes. Otherwise—' she shrugged '—there's nothing he doesn't do very correctly.'

'What are you worried about, then?'

Maggie stared down at her sleeping son with her heart in her eyes. 'I can't help thinking he would be horrified if he knew how—irregular—his situation was.'

She looked up and their gazes clashed.

'Born out of wedlock, you mean?' he said, and for a fleeting moment his mouth hardened. 'That was your choice, Maggie.'

She inclined her head. 'That was before—all sorts of things happened,' she said quietly and ran her fingers along the arm of her wheelchair. 'That was definitely before I came to appreciate the reality of having a baby and what a baby deserves.'

Jack stared at her for a long moment, then he got up and started to push the wheelchair towards the door.

'I can walk or do this myself,' Maggie said.

'Stay put. I need a drink.'

She didn't protest any further and he wheeled her out onto the veranda, and left her to get their drinks. The sun had set, leaving a fiery pattern of cloud and sky to reflect in the calm waters below them.

He came back with a Scotch for himself and a tall

glass of lemon, lime and bitters for her with a sprig of mint in it.

Then he leant back against the railing and studied her. 'What are you suggesting, Maggie?'

She sipped her drink. 'Will you marry me, Jack?'

The silence lengthened between them until he stirred and said, 'Is that what you *really* want?'

What did I expect? she wondered. That he would leap at the idea? That he would declare his undying love for me?

She put her glass down on the veranda table and stumbled up out of her chair.

He caught her on the threshold to the lounge. 'Whoa! Why are you running away?'

'Because you haven't changed one bit,' she flashed at him. 'You never did understand me and you never will.'

He looked down into her anguished eyes, her scarlet face as she tried to pull away. 'Oh, yes, I do.'

'Then why say that, as if—as if it's just another of my mad, impetuous whims?'

'Blame your mother if you want to blame anyone for a desire on my part to be sure of your feelings,' he said harshly.

'My mother!' she gasped. 'What has she got to do with this?'

'A lot. She came to see me after we'd first met at your house.'

Maggie sagged in his arms with disbelief and confusion written large in her expression as she remembered her conversation with her mother about Jack and how she loved him… 'What did she tell you?' she whispered.

He led her towards a settee and they sat down side

by side. 'She told me that you could lead a horse to water but you couldn't make it drink.'

Maggie's mouth fell open.

He smiled briefly. 'She didn't use those words, but that was the gist of it. She told me there was no way I'd get you to marry me unless it was what you yourself had decided to do.'

'She…she really said that?'

He nodded. 'I told her that I had already received that impression and was prepared to bide my time. She then offered me some assistance. Under normal circumstances, she said she would never have dreamt of deserting you in any way, but it would provide *me* the opportunity to provide *you* with some moral support at least and who knew what might come of that?'

'I wondered about that,' Maggie confessed. 'Her going away like that. I put it down to, well, their reconciliation, Mum and Dad's, but I was a bit surprised. I put *that* down to selfishness on my part.'

He lay back and shoved his hands in his pockets. 'I also made a promise to your mother. She can be…' he smiled fleetingly '…a hard woman.'

'I wouldn't have thought that!' Maggie objected.

'Believe me, on the subject of her only daughter, she exhibited some—almost—tigress tendencies.'

Maggie blinked in sheer surprise. 'What did she say?'

'First of all she pointed out the error of my ways to me. To use someone like you as a tool for revenge against your father was diabolical.'

Maggie gulped a breath of astonished air. 'Did you tell her…did you tell her how I followed you and—?'

'No.' He put a hand over hers. 'And it made no

difference; she was *right*. With things the way they were between me and your father, with a girl like you, I was—inexcusable.'

'Was it only revenge?' she asked barely audibly.

He turned his head to her at last. 'Did it feel like it?'

'Not until you sent me away,' she whispered.

His hand tightened on hers until she made a small sound.

'Sorry.' He released her and sat up. 'She then explained that to turn up out of the blue and propose marriage because there was a baby on the way was the height of arrogance even if I still wanted you. And the promise she extracted was that I would stand by you in every other way until, if ever, you discovered I was the one *you* wanted.'

'Oh my,' Maggie breathed. 'Does that mean to say you did still want me? I thought so once, but that was just before Trent was born and it was only once…'

'Maggie—' he rubbed his jaw almost savagely '—I never stopped wanting you. I couldn't get you out of my mind even if I couldn't reconcile—I honestly didn't think I could bring the commitment to a marriage that was needed. There has always been a small part of me that—I don't know—was closed off to that particular traffic. The last nine months have changed all that,' he added.

She was silent, her lips parted, her eyes huge.

'You see,' he went on, 'yes, I cared about my adopted family and Sylvia will always be special to me, but no one has ever walked into my heart and taken it over the way you have.

'No one,' he said quietly, 'brings me the joy and pleasure just in their company you do. And that's one of the reasons I took what turned out to be an increasingly long, hard road these past months. Then there was what you did for Trent. I have never seen anyone battle such painful odds as you did for our son. So you not only have my whole-hearted love, but my utmost admiration, Maggie Trent.'

She wiped her eyes. 'If only you'd told me this sooner—'

He took her hand again, gently this time, but shook his head. 'If there was one thing that finally made me see how much I loved you, it was when your welfare became more important than mine.

'Maggie…' he paused '…sometimes, often, your first love turns out not to be what you think it is at the time. It can be powerful but fleeting, a crush maybe. Also, I had no way of knowing—you possibly had no way of knowing yourself—if you could ever forgive me, or—'

'If it hadn't all been a Maggie Trent, heat-of-the-moment whim?' she suggested gravely.

'I wasn't going to say that.'

'I couldn't blame you if you did.' She gestured.

'What I was going to say was,' he continued, 'there were so many complications it would have been perfectly natural for you to feel dreadfully confused. All I could hope for was that.. time might be on my side. But if it's Trent that's made you come to this decision—'

She put her hand to his lips. 'Jack, I've had my own revelations. I'm a lot more like my father than I dreamt. I'm an all-or-nothing kind of person and that's why I thought it wouldn't work for me with you.'

She hesitated as he kissed her fingers. 'Yes, I

thought I was asking you to marry me for Trent's sake because I didn't know how you felt. But the truth is there's a plus side to the all-or-nothing person I am. I fell in love with you overnight. I will always love you—it may even be a bit of a trial to you at times, but that's me, and it was *always you*, for me.'

'A bit of a trial?' He pulled her into his arms and held her extremely hard as he buried his face in her hair. 'If you only knew how many times I've wanted to do this,' he said on an edge of desperation. 'If you knew how close I came to lowering my guard the night Sylvia rang.'

He lifted his head and looked into her eyes.

She placed a fingertip on the little scar on his eyebrow. 'If you knew what that did to me. Suddenly I was on cloud nine; nothing else mattered!'

'Then…' He hesitated. 'Your back?'

'It's fine, if I take care. Why don't you unplug the phone?'

'Good idea.'

But they didn't go straight to bed. They finished their drinks, he with his arm around her, and they talked.

He told her how he'd manufactured some of his business trips in the last few weeks because actually living in the same place with her had become more of a test of his endurance than he could bear.

She asked him how he felt about her mother now.

He rested his chin on the top of her head for a moment. 'What I said just now was a throwback to earlier times. I may have agreed with her, but there's a certain natural reluctance to think too blackly of oneself.'

She looked up in time to disturb a rueful expression in his eyes.

'I know the feeling,' she agreed.

He kissed her forehead. 'I've made my peace with your mother. To be honest, Trent has to take a lot of the credit for the new state of goodwill between the House of McKinnon and the House of Trent.'

'It's amazing what a baby can do.'

'Mmm… It's just as amazing what his mother has achieved.'

Maggie laid her head on his shoulder. 'I've missed this so much,' she whispered.

He put his other arm around her. 'Me too.'

They sat like that for an age, feeling warm and content, then it grew into more and he started to kiss her.

'The Nile? Or the sands of Araby?'

Maggie looked around Jack's bedroom. It was large, luxurious, but quite impersonal and they were lying on a vast bed, renewing their intimate acquaintance. 'Ah,' she said, 'this is going to take a bit of imagination.'

He looked up. 'I know what you mean. I bought it like this, this place, but it reminds me of a hotel. I haven't got around to changing anything but the den.'

'I could change it for you,' she offered.

'I've had a better idea, I'll tell you about it tomorrow. But talking of change—'

'I know.' She ran her fingers through his hair. 'I've changed a bit.'

He kissed the soft underside of her arm. 'You're still gorgeous. Actually—' he swept his hand down her body and returned it to her breasts '—apart from these, there's not much change at all.'

'All the swimming, gym work and physio has helped enormously,' she told him. 'But you've—lost a bit of weight.'

'I had the feeling I was fading away beneath all that longing for you, Maggie Trent.'

Maggie smiled and kissed the corner of his mouth. 'Well, now you've got me, what do you want to do with me, Jack McKinnon?'

He showed her. He visited all her most erotic spots with his usual care and attention until she was quivering and on fire, and her responses became just as intimate.

'This is going to be quite a ride,' he said with the breath rasping in his throat.

They were lying facing each other. She was in his arms with one of her legs riding high on his thigh.

'It always was,' she murmured.

He brought one hand up to cup her cheek and it was so exquisitely gentle a gesture and there was so much tenderness in his grey eyes, Maggie caught her breath and felt as if her heart could burst with love.

'Now?' he queried.

'Now,' she agreed. 'Yes, please.'

'I thought of a way to do this with the least strain on your back.'

'Oh?'

He rolled onto his back, taking her with him on top of him. 'Not only easy on your back, but you're in total control now, Maggie.'

'Jack,' she gasped as he entered her, 'I'm in no position to… You told me once you were about to die. I'm in the same situation!'

'Hold hard there for a moment, sweetheart,' he commanded, and clamped his hands on her hips. 'We might as well die together. How's that?' he asked as their rhythm co-ordinated.

'Well,' she conceded with a faint smile chasing across her lips, 'that's perfect.'

They said no more until they climaxed together, not only in physical unity but mentally transported as well.

'I love you, I love you, I love you,' she said huskily when she could talk again, with sheer sensual rapture still sweeping her body.

'Me too. I mean I love you, Maggie. When did you plan to marry me?'

She had to laugh, and slowly they came back to earth together. 'Uh—tomorrow?'

Of course it wasn't possible to arrange it that soon, but she got another lovely surprise the next day.

'I'd like to show you and Trent something,' he said the next morning after breakfast. 'We'll take his pram.'

'What is it?'

He studied her. She was feeding Trent and she looked voluptuous, languorous and completely serene. As if she had most satisfactorily been made love to recently, which, indeed, she had.

As have I, he reflected, and I will never let her go again.

'Wait and see.'

'There's a surprise in the air, honey-child,' she told Trent, and Jack grinned.

But her astonishment at his surprise was huge.

'Jack,' she said uncertainly as they stood in the

house on the property that had first brought them together, 'how did this happen?'

The house was no longer neglected. It wasn't furnished, but it had been renovated exactly as Maggie had suggested. It was clean and sparkling and the smell of new paint lingered on the air.

'You told me what you wanted,' he reminded her.

'Yes, but you never mentioned it again!'

'I wanted to do it as a surprise. I thought it might be the perfect place for Trent to grow up.' He took her hand and led her to a window. 'The garden has been cleared and is all ready and waiting for you. I thought you might even like to see if you could grow some *Guettarda Speciosa* here and harvest their perfume.'

'Oh, Jack.' She stood on her toes and kissed him. 'Thank you, from the bottom of my heart.'

He held her close. 'Happy?'

'Yes, very happy. Almost happier than I can bear.' They turned as Trent made a protesting sound from his pram, as if he was taking exception to being ignored.

They linked hands and walked over to the pram.

'We're here, kiddo!' Jack said and they both bent over the pram.

Trent wriggled ecstatically, then he smiled a blinding, toothless smile at them.

Maggie gasped. 'Did you see that—did you see *that*? Do you agree that was a smile and not wind?'

'Sure do. What's wrong with it?'

'He's only two months old! I didn't think it was supposed to happen so early.'

'Maggie—' Jack tossed her a laughing look '—perhaps he's divined that we've got the message and are doing everything by the book now, so he can relax and please himself occasionally?'

MILLS & BOON®

Live the emotion

Modern
romance™

THE DISOBEDIENT VIRGIN *by Sandra Marton*

Catarina Mendes has been dictated to all her life. Now, with her twenty-first birthday, comes freedom – but it's freedom at a price. Jake Ramirez has become her guardian. He must find a man for her to marry. But Jake is so overwhelmed by her beauty that he is tempted to keep Cat for himself...

A SCANDALOUS MARRIAGE *by Miranda Lee*

Sydney entrepreneur Mike Stone has a month to get married – or he'll lose a business deal worth billions. Natalie Fairlane, owner of the *Wives Wanted* introduction agency, is appalled by his proposition! But the exorbitant fee Mike is offering for a temporary wife is *very* tempting...!

SLEEPING WITH A STRANGER *by Anne Mather*

Helen Shaw's holiday on the island of Santos should be relaxing. But then she sees Greek tycoon Milos Stephanides. Years ago they had an affair – until, discovering he was untruthful, Helen left him. Now she has something to hide from Milos...

AT THE ITALIAN'S COMMAND *by Cathy Williams*

Millionaire businessman Rafael Loro is used to beautiful women who agree to his every whim – until he employs dowdy but determined Sophie Frey! Sophie drives him crazy! But once he succeeds in bedding her, his thoughts of seduction turn into a need to possess her...

On sale 4th November 2005

Available at most branches of WHSmith, Tesco, ASDA, Borders, Eason, Sainsbury's and most bookshops

Visit www.millsandboon.co.uk

Look forward to all these ★ ★ wonderful books this ★ Christmas ★

breast cancer CAMPAIGN

researching the cure

The facts you need to know:

- **One woman in nine** in the United Kingdom will develop breast cancer during her lifetime.

- Each year **40,700** women are newly diagnosed with breast cancer and around **12,800** women will die from the disease. However, survival rates are improving, with on average 77 per cent of women still alive five years later.

- **Men can also suffer from breast cancer**, although currently they make up less than one per cent of all new cases of the disease.

Britain has one of the highest breast cancer death rates in the world. Breast Cancer Campaign wants to understand why and do something about it. Statistics cannot begin to describe the impact that breast cancer has on the lives of those women who are affected by it and on their families and friends.

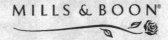

MILLS & BOON®

During the month of October Harlequin Mills & Boon will donate 10p from the sale of every Modern Romance™ series book to help Breast Cancer Campaign in *researching the cure.*

Breast Cancer Campaign's scientific projects look at improving diagnosis and treatment of breast cancer, better understanding how it develops and ultimately either curing the disease or preventing it.

Do your part to help

Visit <u>www.breastcancercampaign.org</u>

And make a donation today.

researching the cure

Breast Cancer Campaign is a company limited by guarantee registered in England and Wales. Company No. 05074725. Charity registration No. 299758.
Breast Cancer Campaign, Clifton Centre, 110 Clifton Street, London EC2A 4HT.
Tel: 020 7749 3700 Fax: 020 7749 3701 www.breastcancercampaign.org

4 FREE

BOOKS AND A SURPRISE GIFT!

We would like to take this opportunity to thank you for reading this Mills & Boon® book by offering you the chance to take FOUR more specially selected titles from the Modern Romance™ series absolutely FREE! We're also making this offer to introduce you to the benefits of the Reader Service™—

- ★ **FREE home delivery**
- ★ **FREE gifts and competitions**
- ★ **FREE monthly Newsletter**
- ★ **Exclusive Reader Service offers**
- ★ **Books available before they're in the shops**

Accepting these FREE books and gift places you under no obligation to buy, you may cancel at any time, even after receiving your free shipment. Simply complete your details below and return the entire page to the address below. You don't even need a stamp!

YES! Please send me 4 free Modern Romance books and a surprise gift. I understand that unless you hear from me, I will receive 6 superb new titles every month for just £2.75 each, postage and packing free. I am under no obligation to purchase any books and may cancel my subscription at any time. The free books and gift will be mine to keep in any case.

P5ZED

Ms/Mrs/Miss/Mr .... Initials ....
BLOCK CAPITALS PLEASE

Surname ....

Address ....

....

.... Postcode ....

Send this whole page to:
UK: FREEPOST CN81, Croydon, CR9 3WZ